"Autumn Winds Over Okinawa, 1945"

"Autumn Winds Over Okinawa, 1945"

Pelham Kenneth Mead III

Library of Congress Control Number:		2011962241
ISBN:	Hardcover	978-1-4691-3399-7
	Softcover	978-1-4691-3398-0
	Ebook	978-1-4691-3400-0

To order additional copies of this book, contact:
Xlibris Corporation
1-888-795-4274
www.Xlibris.com
Orders@Xlibris.com
109122

Contents

Dedication "To my dad who served on the Antietam CVS-36 as a Chief Petty Officer during WWII, who made the one big mistake of getting off on the island of Okinawa that fateful day of August 31, 1945."

On the fateful day on August 31, 1945, four sailors departed the U.S.S. Antietam CV-36 on a launch headed for the shores of Okinawa. The war was officially over, and all of them wanted to transfer back to the States. In the launch were Chief Petty Officer of Machinists, Ken Mead, Seaman First Class Robert Brown, Seaman First Class Lincoln Overland, and Seaman First Class Charles Smitty. The seas were calm that day as the launch headed into the docks at Haku Bay. Atop a flagpole beyond the beach, Old Glory was rippling in the wind. The stumps of hundreds of burned out palm trees were visible beyond the white beach sands. As they approached the beach, they saw battle debris everywhere including American plane parts, and a Jap wing with the red circle on it half sunk in the sand. Huge craters pockmarked the sand where bombs had hit and exploded.

Unbeknown to them this would become their home for over a month despite all their radio efforts calling to nearby ships. It would be a month from hell as two major typhoons hit the island causing massive damage. It would be a month from hell dodging Jap snipers. It would be a month of survival with limited food and water available, since the Navy no longer had a post on the island. All that was left was the Army, and hundreds of Okinawan civilians, and of course Jap snipers, who did not believe the war was over. Insects and disease were as much the enemy as were the Jap soldiers hiding in the limestone caves fighting to the death in honor of the Emperor. This is a story of survival in an unknown incident on the Island of Okinawa at the end of WWII.

Preface

This preface is the author's introduction to typhoons, their origin, background in the Japanese culture, and the extreme damage they can inflict on the island of Okinawa. In this story of survival on Okinawa is the background story of the terrible typhoons that struck Okinawa during WWII in the summer and autumn of 1945.

Autumn Winds from Hell Poem
(By Dr. Pelham Mead, 2011)

Winds of death blow on me,
Winds of death let me be.
Autumn Wind comes so fast,
Whirling death is past.
Circling winds bring pain,
Few escape the heavy rain.
Mountains seem to move,
Trees rip up a groove.
Death comes upon the air,
Settling upon our despair.
Violent terror rages,
Rattling all the cages.
Tents fly high,
Directly to the blackened sky.
Battles in history past,
Seem to be the last.
Winds of War,
Winds that soar.
Release the horsemen of the Apocalypse, too

Red horse, white horse, Black horse and pale horse blue.
Raining death, and famine upon the land,
A windy deadly fighting band.
For the autumn winds of hell,
Will surely ring the bell.
The autumn winds ring loud,
Killing people proud.

In order to understand the terror of a typhoon you have to experience it. Relatively few will ever have to. However, in the summer and autumn of 1945 on the Island of Okinawa, at the end of WWII, several typhoons hit the island, and left a deadly trail of destruction. Typhoons are common to the Pacific and Indian Oceans where the winds can build up over the oceans from warm and cool air and water currents. Hurricanes in the Atlantic do not compare to the might of the Pacific and Indian Ocean typhoons.

A typhoon is defined as a tropical cyclone occurring in the western Pacific or Indian Oceans according to most encyclopedias. It comes from the Chinese word (Cantonese) taaîfung or in (Mandarin) tái, great + Chinese (Mandarin) fast wind. Okinawa has a history of being hit by typhoons every year from June to October, but mostly in early autumn when the weather changes.

History tells us how Japan was saved from destruction by the Mongol Warriors of Kublai Khan's Chinese armies in the 1300s by a typhoon that sank the entire Mongol fleet. The Japanese called this typhoon, "The divine wind." Ironically the Japanese used this same term "divine wind," for their Kamikaze Corps when they sent their suicide pilots to attack the Allies at Okinawa. A typhoon was a divine wind when it did something good for the Okinawans, and Japanese as in the 1300s. So typhoons have both a religious and historical relationship with Japan and Okinawa.

In the last year of WWII, 1945, three major typhoons hit Okinawa in June, September, and October. If the Japanese were waiting for the typhoons to destroy the Allied troops, they were out of luck. The first typhoon hit in June of 1945 arriving too late to help the Japanese fend off the enemy. The battle for Okinawa was already considered over by the end of June. Although the Allied troops received some damage to their ships in June 1945, it was not enough to cause them to lose their advantage over the Japanese defenders on Okinawa. For the Allied forces the battle for Okinawa was over. The kamikazes had sunk hundreds of Allied ships during the spring of 1945 but not enough to help win the battle. The typhoon of June was considered an aftermath of the Battle for Okinawa. The Typhoon of September 1945 only caused the Okinawan people greater pain, and the U.S. Army chaos in their prisoner and civilian compounds and headquarters. The third typhoon of Oct. 9, 1945 was perhaps the worst typhoon of the decade sending the U.S. Army seeking refuge in limestone caves along the southern coast. Again complete devastation was wrought by a massive typhoon with winds up to 150 mph.

A typhoon brings to mind the image of the "Four Horsemen of the Apocalypse" as mention in the bible. The Four Horsemen of the Apocalypse are described (chapter 6:1-8) in the last book of the New Testament of the Bible, called The Book of Revelation of Jesus Christ to Saint John the Evangelist. The chapter tells of a scroll in God's right hand that is sealed with seven seals. Jesus Christ opens the first four of the seven seals, which summons forth the four beasts that ride on white, red, black, and pale horses. Each horseman symbolizes "Conquest, War, Famine and Death," respectively. I used this analogy to best describe what the onslaught of a typhoon is really like. In many ways a typhoon can cause more death than war itself as in the terror of the "Four Horseman of the Apocalypse." It is the innocent who suffer so greatly as did the civilians of Okinawa. Almost 160,000 civilians were killed or committed suicide in 1945. Their deaths are, most of all, the untold story of Okinawa in 1945. Hopefully, this story will relate their suffering and losses during a terrible time in their history.

Chapter 1

The U.S.S. ANTIETAM CVS-36 at Sea
1945

U.S.S. Antietam CV-36 Aircraft carrier 1945

My name is Chief Petty Officer of Machinists Mates, Ken Mead of Brooklyn, New York and this is my story.

I first arrived at the Philadelphia Naval Yard in August of 1944, where the aircraft carrier U.S.S. Antietam CV-36 had just been built. Being a Chief Petty Officer of Machinist Mates, I was a rare commodity stateside since most chiefs had already shipped out and fighting in the Pacific. I was transferred from "Search and Rescue Operations," in Jamaica Bay, New York to the

U.S.S. Antietam CV-36. My job in "Search and Rescue," was to haul the new ninety-day wonder pilots out of the drink whenever they had to ditch a plane. Going on board an aircraft carrier the size of the Antietam was a real privilege for me compared to "Search and Rescue," in a small boat. I thought after a few years in the Navy, that I would never get to see any real war action, but here I was in 1944, two years into the war, ready to board a brand new carrier at the Philadelphia Naval Yard.

The crew on the U.S.S. Antietam CV-36 spent most of the fall of 1944 testing out the U.S.S. Antietam with short shakedown cruises, and training for battle stations, and giving the Navy pilots practice landing on a carrier deck.

The winter months went by fast as we tried to fine-tune the ship. Come spring, May 19, 1945 we had repairs done, and then we were off to Norfolk, Virginia. We stayed for three days, during which time most of the crew had liberty. The weather was beautiful that day and I was glad to get liberty to go ashore and relax with some of the officers.

On May 23, 1945, we departed for Panama, accompanied by the destroyer escorts Higbee (DD-806), Ingram (Apd-43) and the Ira Jeffery (APD-44). The trip was relatively smooth, being that we did not hit any hurricane weather in the Caribbean. I was beginning to get my sea legs, which is an expression related to seasickness and the constant rolling of a ship at sea.

On May 31, 1945, we arrived at Cristobal, in the Panama Canal Zone, and on June 1st we passed through the Canal. It was humid, hotter than hell and very buggy. You could not go on deck without rubbing yourself down with insect repellent. This was the first time I had ever seen the Panama Canal. I cannot imagine how hard it must have been to dig this canal in the old days. It was an exciting time for me.

After exiting the Canal we headed around Baja to San Diego Harbor. We arrived in San Diego on June 10th, and stayed, refueling, and restocking supplies for three more days. San Diego Harbor was a small well-protected harbor with a lot of Navy ships at anchorage. The town of San Diego was a "Navy town," with bars all over the waterfront for sailors and marines. Another first for me being on the west coast. I had never been to LA or San Diego. It was a beautiful little city San Diego.

We had a great time drinking up a storm in San Diego, but on June 13, 1945, we shipped out to Pearl Harbor, Hawaii. The weather was beautiful as usual with some fog in the morning as we left the harbor. On June 19, 1945, we arrived in Pearl Harbor, and started training missions, getting the crew used to manning battle stations and practice shooting at targets in the water.

The sunken ships in the harbor from the Japanese raid were a sad image to see. I had not realized how much damage the Japs had really done to our pacific fleet. Lucky for us three aircraft carriers were out on maneuvers at the time. The U.S.S. Arizona was bubbling oil everywhere from below the surface. We set anchor across the harbor from all the destruction.

We trained off of Hawaii during July 1945. The weather was beautiful most of the time. I did a lot of work on many of the newer planes we had on board. They required constant maintenance. At first I was only familiar with a few planes that I had personally flow back in Floyd Bennet field, but with the excellence maintenance manuals we had it was a constant learning experience. Once you take a plane's engine apart and put it back together, the next time gets easier and easier. Having to teach my mechanists how to work helped to reinforce my knowledge of all the planes we had on board. We had over a 100 planes below deck and could probably handle 200-300 maximum with planes stores on deck and below deck.

On July 19, 1945 we had a major accident. I was working on a Plane below deck when I heard a tremendous explosion that vibrated the entire ship. A 5-inch project had exploded prematurely. One plane was on fire from the blast and several others were damaged. Over a dozen men were injured. This was the biggest accident we had happen since launching the ship last August 1944. Sadly, two or our men died later on from their wounds. Needless to say the Captain was not happy. Our readiness training continued into August 1945.

Being in charge of all the planes and their maintenance was a job of major responsibility. Our biggest repairs were planes that we had to fish out of the drink when they missed the deck on landing. Sometimes we just swapped parts off of one plane, and put it into another plane. Replacement parts were always on order and took forever to be delivered.

We played cards a lot during the down times on board. I had two friends that were in my division that were aviation mechanists 1st class, Seaman Brownie and Lincoln or "Linc," as we called him. They were great mechanists, and I could always depend on them getting the job done right and on time. I always wanted to be a Naval pilot, but I was too old for the Navy Pilot program, so instead I put in as many flying hours so I could to keep up to date with how the planes handled in the air. Landing on the aircraft carrier was the only difficult thing about flying, but I loved the daring challenge. My brother Nate had become a Naval Pilot because he was much younger than myself. Lucky for him, but he never got to leave the states, and remained on the east coast throughout the war.

August 1945 went smoothly with constant training maneuvers to make sure we were ready for combat. Then, suddenly without any warning, the United States dropped a new bomb called an "A" or Atomic Bomb on Hiroshima, Japan on August 6 at 8:15 a.m. from a B-29 bomber flying from a base several hundred miles away at Tinian Islands in the Pacific. The next surprise was on August 9th when a second "A" bomb was dropped on the city of Nagasaki leveling it for 10-15 miles. What the hell was an "A" bomb anyway? We had no idea how deadly this bomb was that it could take out a whole city for a ten-mile radius.

On the same day as the A-Bomb, the Soviet Union invaded Manchuria taking advantage of our preoccupation with Japan. Personally, I did not know what to think when learning of these new "A" bombs that could flatten a whole city. The Soviet Union had once again waited for an opportunity to invade Manchuria when they thought the USA was most vulnerable.

There were a lot of parties that night celebrating our attack on Japan. On August 14th a radio communication came in stating, "The War was officially over at 12:15." What a shock! I remember being on the hangar deck working on a plane when Captain Tague put the radio communication on the PA. All of a sudden there seemed to be no point to being prepared anymore. All that training and not one single sea battle or operation? I had mixed feelings. We put to sea on August 12 bound for the Marshalls. We were three days out of Oahu when we got the official word that the war was technically over and the Japanese had surrendered.

We steamed into Eniwetok Atoll, Marshall Islands on Aug. 19, 1945. Our mission changed from combat to Occupation support duty. We anchored alongside the U.S.S. Intrepid while in the harbor. On Aug. 21, 1945, we had orders to join the Third Fleet to enter into Tokyo Bay. There was a lot of excitement in the air around the ship. We were going to be there for the signing of the treaty.

It was a balmy Pacific day with the usual heat and humidity. On August 21, 1945 we shipped out and set course at 0628. We had a Task Force consisting of U.S.S. Intrepid (CV-11) U.S.S. Cabot (CVL-28), U.S.S. Kimberly ((DD-521), U.S.S. Halsey Powell (DD-686), U.S.S. Allen M. Sumner (DD-692, U.S.S. Obrien (DD-725), U.S.S. Robert t. Hunington (DD-781) and U.S.S. Myles C. Fox (DD-692) a screen of destroyers all bound for Japan. AA gunnery exercises were conducted from 0852 to 1255. My ears were still ringing after gunnery practice. At the conclusion of exercises the task force came to course at 20 knots. Now the urgency was to get to Japan, and try to control all the submarines and other ships that were still ignoring the surrender. There was an atmosphere of excitement around the ship. We were going to see the actual signing of the treaty in Tokyo.

Flight Deck of U.S.S. Antietam CV-36, 1945

We were going to rendezvous with Task Force 38 about 225 miles Southeast of Tokyo. Unfortunately, we had some mechanical problems on the way. With the U.S.S. Ringold, and U.S.S. Harrison, we left formation with orders to proceed to Guam for repairs. What a disappointment that was. I cannot begin to express how depressed all the officers and crew on board were when we realized we had to drop out of the fleet and seek repairs. When they build the aircraft carriers in Philadelphia they did a "rush job," and a lot of the engine set ups and wiring all had to be fine tuned over the past year. We had to head back to Guam for repairs.

Guam is one of the hottest places on the earth. We sailed into to the port at Apra Harbor, Guam for inspections on Aug. 26, 1945. From the minute we anchored in the harbor I began sweating the entire stay. It is a very small sheltered harbor on Guam. All the other ships had already left and just our escort ships and us anchored.

I heard that there was some very loud noises coming from the engine compartment, and the Executive Office J.C. Alderman and the Captain Tague did not want to risk breaking down at sea so we put in at Guam. The inspection party deemed the damage minimal, and the carrier remained operational. What a relief. I thought we were going to be stranded in Guam forever. Thank God we returned to course on Aug. 27, 1945. Now we had lost a lot of time in getting to Tokyo harbor. We were to join the Seventh Fleet at Okinawa with our new orders. Once again we felt we had missed all the action.

Guam Harbor, 1945

Chapter 2

Arriving in Okinawa on Aug. 30, 1945

Early on the morning of Aug. 30, 1945, I could see the Kerama islands with binoculars from the bridge of the U.S.S. Antietam CV-36 aircraft carrier. Captain James Tague had called me up to the bridge to give me my temporary transfer papers that would eventually allow me to be processed for discharge. The Captain handed me the binoculars and said, "Look out there, Chief, those are the Kerama islands that are to the west of Okinawa."

"Thank you Captain," I said and then took the binoculars and scanned the horizon to see many little green islands on the horizon. It was for me, a thrilling sight because now I knew I would be able to get off at Okinawa, and return to Hawaii and then home to Queens, New York. My mind drifted off for a while reflecting on all that I had seen and done in this terrible war.

I had enlisted in the Navy as a Naval Reservist on full time status on July 8, 1941 before the U.S. entered the war. At first I was responsible for "Search and Rescue" in Jamaica bay on Long Island in a small rescue boat. We would retrieve flyers when they crashed in the Jamaica Bay or surrounding areas off Long Island's south shore that were in the approach path to Floyd Bennett Field. When I wasn't doing Search and Rescue, I spent time training as an aviation machinist's mate while at Floyd Bennett Field on Long Island. I was six months too old to become a Navy flyer so I became an aviation mechanic. I always regretted not becoming a flyer but I did get to put in a lot of training hours flying at Floyd Bennett Field for search and rescue operations. This allowed me to at least get a pilot's license that was important in testing out how some of the planes flew after they were repaired. My wife and son (born in June 1942) lived at home with my mother-in-law in Baisley Park, Queens, New York, and a borough of New York City.

It wasn't until four years into the war (August 1944) that I got a transfer as Chief Petty Officer (E7) aboard the newly commissioned aircraft carrier Antietam CVS-36 (commissioned Jan. 28, 1945). I had put in a request to be transferred to the front in the Pacific to see some action rather than spend the remainder of the war state side-fishing pilots out of the water.

U.S.S. Antietam CV-36 at sea 1945

The Antietam was designed after the Essex class (long hull) fleet aircraft carrier. With a displacement of 27,100 tons and a length of 888 ft. she could reach 33 knots top speed. I was transferred in the summer of 1944 to go aboard when the Antietam was launched on August 20,1944. It was built in Philadelphia, and I had to take a train to the Philadelphia Naval yards to get there in time for the launching. I would be in charge of airplane mechanics that would take care of around 100 planes. I remember how shocked I was when I first saw how really huge the ship was while sitting in the Philadelphia Naval yard. It was a day I will always remember. I was nervous with sweat and excited at the same time that I was finally getting to see some action.

After many shakedown cruises and repairs and crew training, the ship was finally commissioned on Jan. 28, 1945. Eventually, the entire crew aboard the Antietam would total around 3448 men.

As of now my enlistment was up, and the war was over as of August 15, 1945 when the Japanese surrendered. It was a great moment for me when Captain Tague thanked me for my service as Chief Petty Officer. I finally started to feel like I had accomplished something in this war.

The islands that surround the western coast of Okinawa dotted the horizon that day. Tokashiki-shima Island, a rather large island, was off to the left on the horizon, and Rukan-sho, a much smaller island was to the right as we approached from the south of Okinawa. The islands looked like small patches of green ovals, much like lilypads on a large pond. There were many other small islands on the horizon that I could not identify as the U.S.S. Antietam CV-36 steamed toward the captured island of Okinawa.

General Douglas McArthur signing the treaty Sept. 2, 1945

The treaty would be signed on Sept. 2, 1945 in Tokyo Harbor on the battleship U.S.S. Missouri, but the Antietam would not be going there for the signing because a mechanical problem back to Guam had forced us to drop out of the fleet that was headed toward Tokyo for the signing ceremony.

Right after the U.S. planes dropped the Atom bomb on Japan on August 6 and 9, 1945, the Russians took advantage of that opportunity and invaded Manchuria. The situation was tense in the Yellow Sea off China and Manchuria. We were redirected to stand off the coast of China in the Yellow Sea after joining the Seventh Fleet at Okinawa, instead of going into Tokyo Harbor for the surrender signing.

When I learned of this at an officer's briefing, I decided I did not want to leave my wife and son at home for another two or three years while I remained off the coast of China. I talked it over with some of my friends, and since the war was officially over my enlistment was also over so I could return to the States, and my family. It all sounded like a good plan.

That was all behind me now for my only thought was "Thank God it is over . . . the war that is." Smitty, a sailor and good friend, a Mechanic's Mate 1st Class was supposed to meet me at 11:00 hours to let me know if he was going ashore on Okinawa. Being a Chief Petty Officer was a big responsibility with roughly 100 airplanes to repair on the ship. I learned to take it in stride even when we got the "ninety day wonder fly boys" onboard who crashed the planes into the deck trying to land. Ninety days was definitely not enough time to learn how to fly, let alone land on an aircraft carrier. They were either crashing into the sea or crashing into the deck. I kept up my flight hours just in case we needed experienced pilots, instead of these rookies.

"Smitty" Charles Johnson Smith, had put in for a transfer to Guam, and wanted to get off at Okinawa to fly back to Guam. Beauvard Browne, "Brownie" another Seaman 1st class, was the first to make up his mind to "cash in his chips," since his enlistment was also up. He wanted to be discharged from the Navy right away before the ship headed into the Yellow Sea for another tour of duty. Like myself he was an older guy in his late twenties. I was 28 at the time, and a few years older than most have the 18 and 19-year-old sailors on board. None of us wanted to stay on the U.S.S. Antietam patrolling the Yellow Sea because that duty would mean not getting back to the States for two or three years or more. It was either get out now, or stay onboard and risk becoming involved in a battle station situation that could go on for a long time off the China coast.

I went below to look for Smitty to see if he had news from the Executive Officer Alderman or Captain Tague about going ashore and leaving the Antietam forever. Smitty was a humorous guy I had gotten to know well since he was assigned to my crew. He was short, 5'6" and had a sun bleached crew cut with a short mustache. He was always being teased about his nose that had a small bulb on the end of it and it was always red. His Irish heritage showed in his temper and redness in his face when he got worked up over something. He was always cursing about something whether it was good or bad.

We were still steaming toward the western side of Okinawa where we would anchor in Nahu Bay near the 9-mile long beaches that were so heavily bombed before the invasion. I found Smitty putting in some zzzzs in his hammock. The Executive Officer J.C. Alderman, said that he would know sometime today whether the Captain had given permission for me to go ashore with Smitty, and Brownie and another guy named Lincoln.

Smitty had been sleeping all morning after doing the night watch. He was eager to get home and so was I. "Chief, do you think we will be in Okinawa before dark?" he asked. I wasn't sure how to respond. "Captain Tague had said he expected to drop anchor by 1430 hours. I'm not sure," I told Smitty. "Maybe we have two hours left in port, somewhere around 1400 hours."

"Did you pack up your duffel bag?" Smitty asked. "Yeah but it was a son of a bitch getting all that junk in one bag. The Captain wouldn't let us take our sea chests, you know," I said. "Yeah, all my tools are in my chest. I hope they can ship it back to the States someday." Just then, Brownie came down the ladder. "Chief, it looks like I am going to be joining you guys going ashore tomorrow." "That's great," I said.

We all began to slap one another on the back, for it seemed like a great moment. Little did we know what we were in for on Okinawa? Another sailor Lincoln Hallard was also going to be leaving with us. The Captain would be providing us with a launch to take us to the beach while the Antietam remained anchored in the bay.

The Antietam had survived the war, and fortunately arrived too late to do battle with the "divine wind," the kamikaze Jap pilots who carried one big bomb, and flew their planes into our ships. We heard all about the battle of Okinawa from radio communications while we were in the Pacific.

Now we were approaching the end of August and the typhoon season in Okinawa. So much had happened so fast over the past year on the Antietam that it seemed like years ago since I boarded. Who would have ever thought we had a bomb like the A-bomb? Who ever thought that we would actually use it against Japan? Strange, I thought, war was more than playing the chess pieces of life and death; it was a story of long waiting hours with little to do. It was a story of constant drills and training to turn a bunch of raw recruits into seasoned sailors. It was a story of accidents like a sailor walking into a plane propeller and having his body spewed all over the ship. It was a story of horror when some sailors misfired a round and blew themselves up. What did we need battles for? We could kill ourselves without the enemy's help.

I often had nightmares of being attacked by a Jap kamikaze and having it dive right into the deck and sinking the Antietam. Sleep was a luxury that I learned never happened in a war, especially on an aircraft carrier where you had to constantly worry about being attacked by planes or submarines.

I had packed my sea bag packed already with all I could jam into it. My leather flight jacket and metal seaman's chest would remain onboard to be transferred back to the States whenever possible after the Manchuria hostilities had ceased.

I said goodbye to some of my crew and some of the officers I got to know while I was stationed on the Antietam. The following day I would be leaving as their Chief and someone else would be taking over after a long year of sailing together. It would be a sad parting since we had grown very close during that time. We played poker all night the last night before I left. I won $355.

On August 30th at about 13:00 hours after a briefing by Captain Tague, Rear Admiral A.C. Davis took over and made the U.S.S. Antietam the flagship of the Task Force 72 including the Interpid and the Cabot. The U.S.S. Antietam was to support the allied occupation forces by a show of air power with planes over North Chin and Korea.

Later on I went back up to the command tower to see if Okinawa was in sight yet. I will never forget when I first saw Okinawa that dreaded afternoon. I was standing on the command tower searching the horizon for the island with my own personal pair of binoculars that I had bought in Hawaii. Yes indeed, it was lying there on the horizon a few miles off. It looked like a long green pea pond in a sea of blue and white water. Almost like a sparkling green paradise island. A fog was rolling in and a light misting rain had begun. The sun had ducked behind some clouds, making the day suddenly very dark. As the U.S.S. Antietam steamed closer I could see the beaches and palms trees. Well not really palm trees; rather burnt stumps that were once palm trees. A green ridge covered with heavy vegetation rose across the middle of the island like the backbone of a lizard. The island was only 60 miles long and two miles wide at some points and seven miles wide at its widest point.

As we approached anchorage in Nahu Bay we went to general quarters. The devastation of the 84-day battle of Okinawa back in the spring of 1945 was apparent with the beaches full of debris from Jap plane parts, boat parts, and bomb craters. I could see that the once pristine white beaches were now black like burnt toast. Bombed out buildings lay along the edge of the beach as a testament to the savage battle. An American flag waved in the wind and rain over an Army headquarters tent on the island back from the beach near a clump of burnt out palm trees stumps. A black cloud moved over the island as if to signal that this was a place of death. As the Antietam moved into the harbor area a stench of ammunition, burnt wood and an undefined acid smell pervaded Nahu air. I couldn't get over the complete look of devastation on the island from the sea. It was as if all the armies and navies of the war had dumped their garbage on the beach. What a mess!

It would not be until 11:00 the following morning on August 31st that Smitty, Brownie, Lincoln and I would be allowed to go ashore in a launch. I will never forget going down over the side 65 feet or more on a rope cargo net holding a 80-pound plus duffel bag. One of the ship's boatswains sounded the boatswain's pipe as an act of respect as we left the ship. It gave me a chill in my spine that I was leaving my floating home and preparing to return home. Dropping over the side of the ship from the elevator was like the drills they used to do in Navy training camp in 1941. The drop over the side was steep and my duffel bag strap was digging into my shoulder numbing my arm completely. Each step down the cargo net was painful, but I finally made it to the bottom into the waiting Launch with a small outboard engine. Smitty could not climb down with his bag, so he yelled, "Chief, catch my bag, it is too heavy."

Like a fool I said "OK" and I reached out to receive a crushing force on my arms from a duffel bag, which must have weighed 200 pounds. "What do you have in this bag, stones," I yelped. Just the four of us, Smitty, Brownie, Lincoln and myself went ashore that day. My crew was on the deck waving to me as we headed for the beach. I looked back and waved with a twinge of sadness to see my floating home fade behind us in the distance. We took an extra bag of mail for the Army and Navy guys on shore. Little did we know that the Navy had pulled out of Okinawa and was preparing for the surrender signing in Tokyo Harbor and rounding up any stray submarines who did not hear the war was over.

Chapter 3

The Day we landed on the Nahu Beach at Okinawa, Aug. 31, 1945

It took about 10 minutes to get to the shore with the launch. The waves were high that day, and a lot of shipwrecks had masts jutting out of the water in the shallow areas. We beached the boat and pulled our gear and mail sack ashore. We thanked the sailors who had brought us ashore and saluted as they shoved off on their return to the Antietam.

There was no greeting party or soldiers or sailors there to greet us. In fact, it was uncommonly quiet except for jungle birds that were chirping up a storm. A light rain began to increase blowing like a mist over the entire island. There was the smell of smoke in the air mixed with the acid rot odor of dead bodies. To think, here we stood on Nahu Beach where thousands of American Marines and Infantry had come ashore unopposed by Japanese forces on April 1, 1945.

The cold rain was increasing and making it difficult to see beyond the overhead low hanging clouds and dense fog. Garbage was everywhere on the beach. Pieces of ships, and planes were strewn around everywhere like seashells of war. Instead of the white sands being smooth, they were as cratered as the surface of the moon. It was difficult walking across the beach to the edge of the jungle area where burnt out palm trees formed an almost impenetrable field of debris.

Our plan was simple, try to get the first boat out of Okinawa going back to Hawaii where we could then be discharged. Smitty was being transferred to Guam and had orders to fly out in two days. He would be flying out of a little field just above Nahu. Nahu was a city just to the south of the beaches we landed on that was completely flattened by naval bombardments prior to the landings of the Army and Marines invading on April 1, 1945.

There were few other boats in the harbor except the Antietam, and the Intrepid, the Cabot, and two escort battleships, so the return boat option did not seem likely with these ships since they were all going to the Yellow Sea off the coast of China. Way down the beach to the south was an American flag waving in the rain over a huge Army headquarters tent. It was a good long walk along the beach to the Army camp, so we threw our duffel bags over our shoulders and shuffled slowly through the sand and war debris. I actually stepped over a piece of a Jap Zero's wings with the well-known orange circle insignia on it. It was probably a remnant of a kamikaze plane that crashed into a ship or the ocean. By the time we got to the Army encampment we were dragging the bags through the sand. When we came upon the 10th Army headquarters we asked where the Navy was stationed and we were informed that the Navy had pulled out of Okinawa several days before in August. That was one of our first strokes of bad luck. The division of the 10th Army stationed there didn't exactly welcome us. They had other duties to do and we were just in the way.

Army Sergeant Stanton who was in charge of the company C stationed at the southern end of Nahu Beach had given us permission to use several empty tents. After we went through some paperwork, we slowly dragged our sea bags into the tents and moved an extra bunk in so we could all stay together. We spent the rest of the day going over rules and restrictions outlined by Sergeant Stanton. He was a short squat guy with tattoos all over his arms. He was almost completely bald and kept his hat on most of the time to protect him from the tropical sun. He had one of those roaring belly laughs when something struck him as funny and our predicament with not having any Navy stationed on the island amused him. I noticed a huge Eagle tattoo on his army with an American flag behind on his left arm. He was really quite the character.

Sargent Stanton laughed, and said, "OK Chief you and the swabbies are stuck here for a while and we have little or no rations for you. You need to stay within the protected area and if you venture out the password is 'Abraham Lincoln Brigade.'" Passwords were always selected with combinations of R and L because it was difficult for Japs to make these sounds correctly.

"OK Sarg," I said, "we don't want to be here any longer than necessary and will stay our of your hair." "That suits me fine," the Sergeant said with a laugh. He amused easily, at our expense it seemed. Just then I saw a flash of light come out of the jungle and my first instinct was to drop to the ground, but before I could do that I heard the crack of a sniper rifle, and I knocked the Sergeant to the ground as I dropped. A bullet whistled overhead and struck the palm stump behind the tent we were standing in front of. "Boy, that was close, Sarg, sorry I knocked you down," I said.

Startled and brushing off his pants the Sargent got up and grabbed for his walkie-talkie. "Bud, get three men with rifles out near that perimeter, and get that sniper one way or another," he barked. Turning to me he said, "Thanks, Chief, I owe you one. I guess you saved my life." We were the best of friends from that day on. Sargent Stanton talked to the Captain for me, and we were allowed to stay in the camp until a ship or plane returning to Hawaii picked us up. It was a twist of fate that both worked for us, and against us, as I was to find out after weeks without rescue.

The Army was not obligated to feed or protect us since their assignment was to secure the island and to round up Okinawan civilians, search for unexploded shells and capture any remaining Japanese soldiers. We were not part of their master plan. There was a major miscommunication between the Navy and the Army in this situation and we were caught right in the middle.

The Army never offered to feed us and we realized this was going to be a difficult stay on the island without a food supply. Sarg Stanton became our ally, and got foods to us whenever he could without the Captain knowing about it. To get food we would have to barter for it or win it playing poke or ace deuce (a game like backgammon). I was one of the best poker players on our ship of 3,000. Needless to say we were forced to play a lot of poker to get the water and food we needed to survive. It didn't seem long-term at the time because we were still confident at that time that we would be leaving in a few days and taking a plane or boat back to Hawaii. "Smitty, you better check with the radio man and see when the next ship is coming by to pick up Brownie and I," I said.

"It's okay, Chief; I already have a confirmation on a plane coming into the airstrip near here, which will fly me to Guam. You guys are welcome to take a vacation on Guam if you want," Brownie said. "No thanks," I said.

The first night on the island was difficult after being on a ship for so long. (About a year since the ship first hit the water on August 20, 1944). I was still rolling form side to side in my bunk as if I was still in my hammock on board the ship. A few shots rang out in the night followed by some shrieks. I tried to focus in my sleep on returning home to see my four-year-old son and wife. I slept little that night. Brownie and Smitty had the same problems. The stench of death was everywhere in the air and in our dreams. "Brownie, did you hear that shot," I whispered. "Yeah Chief, I heard it, sounds like someone is hunting down those Japs." "Just so long as they don't decide to make the headquarters here a target gallery is fine with me," I said. Smitty put in a few words. "Hey,

Chief, don't worry we have some blankets we can tie them up with if they rush us." "Ha." I laughed. "You are a funny guy, Smitty."

I was able to relax a little more after that and the night swept by gunshots and all. The bugs bit at me all night long flying into my ears, and buzzing before I smacked my ear and killed them. The bugs crawling around the ground and the tent were huge. This was definitely not paradise. The cockroaches were really large and scary. It really surprised me when I saw one crawling across the deck. They were as big as palmetto bugs found in Florida. I smashed the bug with my shoe. All night long I could hear them running across the tent's wooden floor. In addition to the centipedes that ran six inches long, and the geckos that looked like cute little lizards that chirped and used suction pads for feet and could hang off the wall or ceiling with ease. We were warned about the Habus, which were two kinds of poisonous snakes that can be found in the caves and sugar cane fields. I was told that a Habus snake could swallow a huge banana spider in one gulp.

As morning fog began to lift, the island was still shrouded in a gray mass of what looked like oatmeal in the sky with the rain still drizzling. We went to the mess tent to find that the Army had very few provisions and they did not want to share any with us. Fortunately, we had all stuffed whatever K-rations and food we could find into our sea bags.

We did not have enough to survive beyond three days or so. Poker would be our ace in the hole in winning food that the army would not volunteer to give us. Getting off the island quickly would be our best chance to survive. "Well, Chief, I hope you brought the poker cards along from the ship," said Brownie. "Right in my pocket, laddie," I said. "I can't remember when you last lost a hand, Chief," said Smitty as we walked of the mess tent. "You're right," I said. "I haven't lost in months so I hope my good luck streak continues." Smitty talked to a few soldiers and had set up a Navy vs. Army poker game for the night. It would be our chance to win some food.

The U.S. marines had left in July 1945 to become part of the invasion force on the other Japanese islands before the surrender was declared. The Navy had some supply stations on land for a while but had long since left the island to prepare for the invasion of Japan. Unfortunately, no one informed us, or many of the other naval vessels of this departure. It was traditionally the Army's job to take care of the occupation of an area after the battles were over and the island or country was declared seized.

I couldn't help but notice that there were graves everywhere on or near the beach and around the outside of the army tent area. Sticks marked some graves and others were small mounds in the sand with stones on top of them. The

Four Horsemen of the Apocalypse had truly used their swords of destruction to bring death and famine to this island. We were warned that malaria and dengue were everywhere on this island in addition to many other tropical diseases that had no name. Dengue is also called breakbone fever, and if you get it your bones feel like they are in a vice, and someone is twisting the vice on you.

The Okinawan civilians were nowhere to be found. They were still hiding in the bushes in the interior and in the many caves that dotted the island. Some Army private told me they committed suicide by the thousands in fear of the Americans raping, torturing and killing them as they were told by the Japanese propaganda. Some Okinawan and Japanese soldiers were still hiding out in caves believing the war was continuing. It sounded like a very sad story for the original inhabitants of the island. They were caught between the Japanese Imperial Army and the Allied forces invading the island. The discussions at all the meals were about the Battle of Okinawa and how the conditions were horrible.

On one hand the Japanese tortured and killed thousands of Okinawans and forced any able-bodied teenagers and young women into the Imperial Japanese army to fight for the Emperor. The other side of the scenario seemed just as bad in falling victim to the American invaders who also seemed like monster killers. It was one of the missions of the U.S. Army soldiers stationed on Okinawa to flush out the Okinawan civilians, and Japanese soldiers from caves and bushes and put them in tent cities set up by the Army. Captured soldiers were treated as prisoners of war and put in a detention camp separate from the civilian camp. Here the Army could feed the civilians and attempt to gain their trust. The camps were not pleasant with barbed wire all around just like any prison camp. I wondered whether the barbed wire was to keep them in or prevent the Japs from

The barbed wire compound where the Okinawan civilian were kept

Attacking? Old women and half naked young children and old men were all that survived the battle. They laid around the tent compounds like they were in a trance. None of the American soldiers trusted them because they were told some of them could be Japanese soldiers in disguise.

On the morning of day two each of us were devouring an exciting can of k-rations baked beans for breakfast. "Want some eggs, Chief?" Smitty called over to me. "Sure," I said. "Where are you going to get them?" "We could hunt for some birds or chickens or something," Smitty said. "There must be some chickens around here somewhere," he remarked. "Yeah, sure, we are going to go through those dense jungles looking for chickens only to get shot by a Jap or step on a land mine." Suddenly from some low bushes about 50 yards away from our tent, a Japanese soldier came running out of the bushes screaming, "Bonsai" as he dashed across the sand at us.

I had left my officer's revolver in my duffel bag, so I stood there helpless as the enemy soldier charged the camp with a rifle aimed at us. He had two hand grenades tied to a string hung around his neck. The Army guys that were in the tent next to us picked up their rifles and gunned the Japanese soldier down before he could clear 50 feet. That was the first time I saw someone shot down. The Army guys explained that the Japanese were instructed to fight to the death for the Emperor, and refused to give up. During the "mop up operation" in late June and early July of 1945 the American soldiers went out and hunted down the Japanese like they were hunting rabbits. They took no prisoners and just shot all the Japs they could find. They torched them out of caves, threw hand grenades in other caves or shot them down in open fields as they ran away. "Holy crap, did you see that," I said. Smitty and Brownie were still frozen sitting on their bunks unable to move.

Right after that incident we went to Sarg Stanton and had rifles distributed to us. The soldiers had to throw a grenade at the dead Jap to set off the grenades he was wearing around his neck. Only a pool of blood remained after all of the grenades exploded around his neck and the one thrown by the American. It made me lose my appetite completely and I had to sit down because I was feeling sick.

War is hell and this war of attrition or "jikyusen" as the Japanese called it, became a manhunt to clean out any enemy combatants hiding in the underbrush or caves that dotted the island. Many Okinawans fell victim to the manhunt also since the Americans could not tell who was an Okinawan civilian and who was a Japanese soldier. After that day I kept my officers pistol strapped to my side. I only had around fifty rounds of ammunition but I loaded my pistol and kept extra shells in my pocket. I never forgot that we were still in a war zone even though the war was officially over.

For the rest of the day Brownie and I kept the radio operator, Private Charlie Debree of Company C, busy trying to arrange for someone to pick us up off the island. Smitty had a R4D plane arranged to fly him to Guam where he was transferring and he would be leaving at 1300 hrs. The following day, Brownie, Lincoln, and I still could not get a flight or a boat of any kind out of Okinawa. We were like a forgotten island. It was very frustrating. We had thought that we would be on this burned out island for only a day before being transported out. We seemed to be heading in the wrong direction from everyone else, away from Japan instead of toward Japan.

U.S. Ships anchored in Nahu harbor 1945

The following day Smitty left in a jeep with two other infantry guys to drive to the Kadema airfield near Nahu and he flew out to Guam leaving Brownie, and I to survive alone. He left with five injured U.S. Army soldiers who had been wounded by landmines, snipers and armed civilians. Brownie and I went along for the ride and to say goodbye to a friend. Smitty gave us what K-rations he had left since we were low on food and had to sneak into the Army mess tent and steal food in the night.

For the first few days of September 1-2,1945 most ships were headed toward Tokyo and the Yellow Sea and none were returning to Hawaii. It began to sink in to our thick skulls that we were trapped on the Island of Okinawa for much longer than we wanted to be.

After the signing of the peace treaty on Sept 2, 1945 we celebrated with the Army soldiers with two cans of beer rationed out to each of us. We were glad to get the fluids even if it was beer. Bad weather was predicted during the month of September, which was typhoon season on Okinawa. They were known to have major typhoons that rocked the island and everything on it. The Army radio operator, Charlie got a message from Hawaii central that a typhoon was forming off the coast and moving toward Okinawa in the next week or so. It might hit the island around the 10th of September or so. Now the "C" Company would need every able-bodied man to move all the tents and equipment to higher ground and seek shelter other than tents. A tent would be no shelter during a storm of such magnitude, so we accompanied the Army soldiers in search of some safe secured caves where we could weather out the typhoon. The Okinawan civilians who numbered around 1,000 had to be moved also. We used an interpreter by the name of Nayoshi to ask the Okinawans where the closest caves were. Most of them were far south of the beaches. Most of the caves were along the southern shore of the island, which was a long drive from the Nahu beaches. We would have to pass through the now destroyed city of Nahu, once the capital of Okinawa and search for caves along the ridges to the south. The caves dotted the cliffs above the southern Okinawan seashore because of the limestone formations. The first cave we came across near the road heading south had some Okinawan civilians hiding in it. We shouted into the cave, "Konnichiwa" meaning hello in Japanese. At first there was no reply. It was obvious someone was living in the cave since clothing was hanging from a string attached to the side of the cave. Again we called into the cave, "Konnichiwa, watashi Wa American soldier desu, shusshin wa doko-desuka?" Which roughly translates to, "Hello, I am an American soldier, do you speak English?"

They came out with their hands over their heads after we shouted our broken Japanese phrases into the cave. Five of them ran right off the jagged cliffs to their deaths on the rocks below. It was a chilling and disgusting sight. One of the Okinawans was a little girl about age five and she and four other older women lay dead on the rocks with the ocean waves lapping over them. They had finally achieved peace at the cost of their own lives. It was hard for us soldiers to understand how the Okinawans thought. There was an equal mistrust on both sides. The remaining old men, women and young children of about 20 or so Okinawans came out with their eyes down and their hands folded together in a praying position. Several MPs took them and gave them some water and K rations and drove them back to the stockade, where all Okinawan refugees were being kept until the Army could decide what to do with them.

We had Nayoshi call out in Japanese for anyone else hiding in the cave to come out. No one came out at out but Nayoshi was afraid to enter the cave for fear of stepping on a boobie trap or land mine. The U.S. Army Captain Tillen, who commanded the C company, gave the order to throw a grenade in first and then torch the cave. The GI with the flamethrower let go with a blast of fire throughout the mouth of the cave. No one came out, so we proceeded into the cave cautiously. The ceiling was about 12 feet high and the cave looked to be more than 30-40 feet deep with boulders and lots of small burnt vegetation growing up the sides of the cave. We found four Japanese soldiers lying dead behind a boulder in the cave with knives in their stomach, hara-kiri style. We removed the bodies and radioed back to the camp to move some of the supplies into the cave so we could take shelter in the cave during the typhoon. We spent the next two days helping the Army guys move radio equipment, ammunition and food into the cave and many other caves nearby, which were many miles from the camp.

The most difficult thing to watch was the Okinawans being put onto transport trucks and moving them back to the refugee stockade with the MPs. They reminded me of cattle being rounded up for slaughter. During the typhoon they would be a lot less safe in the tents than where we were taking refuge. The area just off the beach where the stockade was located was beginning to swell with hundreds of Okinawan refugees and it stunk to high hell since no latrines were available nor running water or any other conveniences. Later on when it was obvious the civilians would not be safe near the beach area a plan was made to truck them to large caves for shelter and safety along the shore below Nahu the city to the south of Hagushi Harbor.

The infantry guys rewarded us with some of their valuable rations for helping move their equipment. They also shared some awamori, an Okinawan form of liquor. Awamori is made from crushed rice that is fermented for about two weeks. I have never seen Army cooks make a more disgusting mess by mixing several cans of K rations together and calling it a meal. The soldiers called it, "Shit on rye bread." We were so hungry we could have eaten roast rat if we had to. It was the water we had to watch out for. None of the local water could be consumed due to many tropical diseases that could easily make a quick death look better.

Already I had contracted some tropical disease since my gums were bothering me and they were bleeding a lot. I used what little I had of a bottle of scotch to kill the pain and bleeding. Each day my teeth were getting looser and bleeding all the time. I lost three teeth already since my gums were inflamed and all my teeth were loosening up. I took pain pills practically every day. I began to live on them after a while since I could not overcome the pain and bleeding.

Aspirin only made the gums bleed easier from thinning the blood out so I was forced to get other types of medication from the medics. "Linc" was complaining about cuts he got on his feet when he was walking barefoot on the beach. Lots of glass and metal were buried in the sand and it was dangerous to walk without shoes. Lincoln had two infections on his right foot so bad he had to limp a little in order to walk. I kept telling him to have the medic give him a shot to kill the infection.

The first time I realized I caught some kind of jungle disease that was when I went to clean my teeth with a toothbrush and a tooth fell out. Jungle diseases and bugs were the real silent enemy, not the Japs. The bugs were getting the better of us too. Spiders were the size of your fist, flies were everywhere, and mosquitoes were as long as your fingers, like Jersey mosquitoes. I had to rub gasoline on my skin since I had no bug repellant and neither did Brownie. He had a nasty infected bug bite, which the Army medic took care of by applying straight iodine solution.

With the beginning of each day I headed to the radio shack to see if any ships were putting into Nahu bay and continuing onto Hawaii. Our stay on Okinawa was beginning to become a survival ordeal. What I thought would be a quick turnaround, and back to Hawaii was becoming a grueling struggle for survival on a Jap infested island in the Pacific. Each day we would radio for any ships nearby but got no response. Still the acid odor of death hung in the air everywhere. I was beginning to wonder if we would ever get off this island of hell. My health, Lincoln, and Brownie's was starting to take a turn for the worst. We had to eat what we could get our hands on and most of the time it was high carbohydrate K rations. We began to talk about getting some local food from the fields where sweet potatoes or rice were being grown.

When we occasionally ate with the Army guys and we heard story after story of what went on during the Battle of Okinawa. First there were 100,000 Japs and then there were 70,000 Japs and civilians defending the island. The stories got bigger and bigger as the days went along. I found that I was beginning to dream about General Fujijima of the Japanese 32nd Army and his Chief of Staff Cho. The ghosts of the Japanese Generals and staff officers that committed hara-kiri in that cave opening on June 21, 1945 were everywhere on the wind, in the trees and especially the dark clouds and fog at night. I had nightmares every night of Japanese soldiers killing themselves with knives and having their heads sliced off like baloney with sammauri swords so they did not suffer too long.

The hot and humid Okinawan days seemed to drag on and on. Would this nightmare ever come to an end?

Japanese General Ushijima of the 32nd Japanese Army on Okinawa

Chapter 4

Asao-Sam Boy

Our Okinawan buddy Asao, "Sam-Boy"

We had to be very careful where we walked outside of the secured camp area. Many undetonated bombs from the battle area dubbed "iron hurricanes," were frequently found in bushes, beaches and practically anywhere on the island. There were also personnel land mines buried in and along the roads.

Our safest deal was to stay with the Army as they patrolled around the beach area south of Nahu Bay, and further south to Nahu, and inland to Shuri ridge and the remains of the Shuri Castle.

Searching the surrounding areas for Japanese soldiers who were still hiding or posing as Okinawan civilians was the 10th Army's major task. It wasn't until Sept. 7th that a whole division of Japanese soldiers surrendered at the nearby Kedama airport. Still the danger was not gone since now all of the remaining soldiers were cut off from any officers or official staff to inform them of what to do besides fight to the death and never surrender.

Sometime during the second week we were on Okinawa, I saw a young boy walk out of the bushes along the ridge road near the Army tent compound with his hands over his head. He was wearing torn and ragged clothing. He looked like he had just stepped out of a David Copperfield novel. I was driving an Army jeep helping to move supplies to the caves we were using to protect us from the impending typhoon. Just to the left of the Okinawan boy was a half exposed shell that had not been detonated. We waved the boy away from the shell, and then hid behind a large boulder several yards and threw a grenade at the shell. The first grenade bounced off a nearby rock but the second one was right on target. What an explosion. The huge ten-foot boulders we were hiding behind actually cracked from the explosion. Lucky we covered our ears because the explosion was enough to cause serious hearing loss.

Whenever these shells exploded they threw metal fragments for yards in every direction and anyone unfortunate enough to be within a short distance from the shell never had a chance. The metal would cut them in half or tear them down to a pile of flesh in but a second. The small Okinawan boy screamed from fright and shouted something in Japanese, and collapsed crying on the ground. He was about 8 or 9 years old and was filthy from having not bathed in months. We offered him a candy bar. He thanked us in Japanese for saving his life or at least I think that is what he said since, "Konnichiwa," was all I could understand in my limited knowledge of Japanese. He took the candy bar and greedily ate. I tried a little of my broken Japanese with the little boy, "O-namas wa nan-desu-ka?" which roughly means what is your name?

His response was, "arigatou, watashi no Nama WA Asao desu." The rough translation was 'my name is Asao.' I decided to call him Sam-boy. I lifted him up on the jeep, and he rode on it until we got back to U.S. Army compound. We found a young Okinawan woman in the refugee tent city to take care of him. Later that day Sam boy told the MPs that he was our personal assistant, and was allowed to leave the Okinawan civilian secured area each day and come to the Army compound, and beg for food. We built up a close relationship as Brownie, Lincoln, and I taught him English expressions, and he taught us Japanese expressions. It helped to pass the time when some days we had no radio contact with any vessels going south to Hawaii. "Sam boy," I said, "these are cards, you play cards?" He nodded. I spent a lot of free time showing him the cards and the English name for each card. Teaching him Poker was a little more difficult. "No, Sam boy, that is a King, pair of kings better than pair of 10's," I said. Over and over we played and it passed away the hours.

Surprisingly there were always ships at anchor off Okinawa but none of them were going to Hawaii. They were all focusing on Japan, and the China problems in the Yellow Sea. Many of the ships transporting soldiers back were already overflowing and to stop for just three sailors didn't seem to justify the problem of anchoring, sending in a boat and wasting several hours in cruise time.

10th U.S. Army patrols the ruins at Nahu 1945

We went through Nahu several times but it was nothing but crumbling shells of building structures. Few walls were left standing from the barrage of American battleship bombardment. A temple was left partially standing, and the wall of a university was still standing but the rest of the city was rubble. We found a few shells stuck in the ground and so we very cautiously detonated them by using hand grenades or rolling them off a cliff to explode on the rocks below.

There was no food to be had anywhere, no rice, no sugar cane, nothing. Just burned out fields of sugar cane remained, and rice paddies that no longer had water in them from bomb craters that destroyed the levies that once held the water in. The rubble from Nahu was everywhere and no civilians were to be seen anywhere. It was a city of death. Brownie and Linc traveled in one Army Jeep and I traveled in another as we bumped from one shell crater to the next.

My back and neck were killing me from the constant jolting of the shelled out road to Nahu. It was slightly to the south of where our beach encampment was located and a long hour ride because of the pockmarked road, mud and unexploded shells. The caves were beyond Nahu down the coast. "Linc did you find any food?" I asked. "No Chief all the vegetable crops are ruined and we could not find any hidden stores of food," said Linc. "Well keep looking Linc and maybe we will find something," I said. Food was scarce everywhere.

Between the bugs and the humidity I was miserable more and more each day. Radio contact would be dead silent someday when it came to ship activity. Everything was centered on Tokyo, 300 plus miles to the north and the Yellow Sea area to the west. When we returned from the caves in the early evening, standing there on the edge of camp was Sam-boy as I called him. The Army sentries would not allow him in the secured camp area. I told them it was OK and that I had given the kid some candy bars earlier in the day. I told him to go home but he shook his head as if to say, no. Brownie went to get the Army interpreter so we could communicate with the little guy. We talked with him at length and I decided it would be ok if we let him come back to our tent with us. I had to get permission from the Sergeant Stanton first. He was reluctant at first, and said the kid should be put in the Okinawan civilian stockade, but relented when I pointed out that he could be useful as another interpreter and guide around Okinawa. The compromise was he still had to return home at night to the Okinawan refugee stockade. We tried to give him some food we could spare.

It was near the end of the third week of our stay on Okinawa that we realized that Kadena airport was a virtual stockpile of supplies for the original plan to invade Japan from Okinawa. I had seen the tires and ammo cases stacked near the beach Army compound but did not realize that the Army and Navy had already stockpiled materials during July, and early August 1945.

The U.S. Army compound on Okinawa 1945

Back at our tent and we had a small package of peanut butter and a package of crackers, a banana and a new 10-gallon water container with fresh water brought in by the many container ships in the bay. Rations were getting low for a while, but now daily supplies were arriving to help the U.S. Army, and the refugees who were beginning to come out of the caves and hills where they were hiding for the past year or so. I gave a few crackers I could spare to Sam-boy who stayed outside the tent. Brownie wanted to know what we were going to do with the kid. I had no answer. I was too tired to think about it. I have been teaching him Poker, I said.

As soon as my head hit the cot I was sound asleep with soldiers and civilians running across fields shooting at one another in my dreams. I awoke the following morning to an explosion that rocked the camp. I fell onto the ground under my bunk. The little Okinawan boy was hiding under the cot also crying aloud. I could see the look of panic on his face. I reached under my cot for my officer's pistol and looked around to see where the explosion came from. Just then I heard a whistle being blown and a soldier yelling, "All clear!" Brownie and I ran over to the main tent to find out what was going on. "What the hell was that?" I shouted. Lincoln was already there talking to another G.I. Sam-boy ran along behind me. Apparently a Japanese soldier crawled out of the bushes with two hand grenades strapped to his head. The sentries tried to shoot him before he could get too close to the camp. He pulled the pins himself and the grenades went off not causing any damage to the U.S. Army compound at about 100 yards from the camp. There was nothing left of the Jap soldier except some pieces of clothing stained with blood.

"It's Ok, Chief," one of the infantry guards said, "he's oatmeal now." I wanted to throw up but I didn't have anything in my stomach. I looked out at the clearing near the camp and all I could see was a small hole, some pieces of clothing and blood splattered everywhere. The tents nearest the explosion were dotted in red. I was like someone dropped a balloon from the sky full of house paint. A grenade could really do a lot of damage and in this case it was two grenades. It made me sick.

I had lost 12 pounds or more in just a few weeks. Lincoln lost 10 pounds and Brownie lost about 8 pounds. Finally the Army was getting more and more food and rations on a daily basis. Supply ships came in almost every day to re-supply the Army companies still stationed on Okinawa. Most of the stockpiles of supplies were up by the Kadema airport inland nearby since the U.S. was storing supplies during July for the assault on Japan that was planned for August and the fall of 1945. The Atomic bombs saved that possibility by bringing the Japanese to their knees.

Sam-boy became a fixture around our tent. He could speak broken English but was able to communicate with his hands a lot better. His favorite expression was "Yanks . . . or Ken-son." Several Okinawan women came to the compound every day to clean up the officer's mess tent and to work as cooks and domestic help in the menial tasks of keeping a compound clean. Quonset huts were being erected and more and more supplies and central offices were being established.

Sam-boy told us his story about what happened through one of the Okinawan women translating for him. His sisters were all raped and pushed off the cliffs by Japanese soldiers and American bombing and naval shells flattened his house in Nahu. The Japanese shot his parents when they refused to leave their house and go with the Japanese into the interior of the island. He hated the Japanese and was afraid of the Americans at the same time, but had no one to live with. The Okinawans looked upon him as another mouth to feed and turned him out on his own to survive. He was one of thousands of orphans with no family alive and no home to go to. He said he had been eating wild fruits and plants and had caught some fresh water fish by himself with a wooden stick. He had been alone for over four months living in the bushes and small caves big enough for one small person. He said he had to stay away from the large caves because Japanese occupied most of them. The food I gave him convinced him that Americans were not the "dog-faced Yankee white devils" that Japanese preached.

One of the Army's missions was to convince the Okinawan civilian people to come out of hiding and that the war was over and they would be safe. That was an impossible mission in lieu of all the propaganda they had heard from the Japanese about the "killer pig Americans." Sam-boy could be an ally in helping us accomplish that goal of talking to the Okinawans and trying to gain their trust by giving free food supplies and shelter. More and more each day we brought Sam-boy with us on every mission to seek out civilians and get them to return to tent cities the army had established. I almost forgot for a while that I wanted to go home. There was so much healing to be done on this island of hell. Sam-boy was a big help and funny in a lot of ways in which our cultures clashed. My Japanese improved by constantly talking to him in Japanese phrases. We fed him with whatever food we had left over. Sam-boy taught us how to pick rice in rice paddies and dry it. I had never picked rice before, but I was starved all the time and rice would be a helpful addition to our one small meal a day. The rice paddies were mined also and we had to be very careful. Anyone out in the open was subject to a Jap sniper killing him or her. No open area was safe. Our k-rations had run out and we were dependent on the Army generosity in giving us food or we had to steal it without permission at night. We were planning to make a raid or barter trip to Kadema airport where tons of American supplies were stockpiled. All we needed was something the Quartermasters needed to trade with. Whiskey was a sure bet for a trade and we had several bottles we had all bought in Hawaii when we were running training drills there back in July 1945. We were in a difficult position not being officially part of the Army and being in Navy limbo at the same time. As far as the Army or Navy were concerned we were in transit and not officially out of the service yet. The jungle rot was getting to us, bug bites, and mold forming on our clothes and body from the humid and wet conditions. My bleeding gums were getting worse and more teeth had already fallen out. I was beginning to get worried. Lincoln's foot infection seemed to never go completely away despite all the antibiotics he was taking. The Army medic gave me some general antibiotics, which seemed to help, but I knew I caught some kind of jungle disease that would never go away before all my teeth fell out. When the hell were we going to get out of this place, I asked myself? I had some kind of jungle disease on my skin on my left arm. My skin was drying up and always itchy. Okinawa and it's humid weather was beginning to take it's toll on all of us.

I went down to the radio shack as I did everyday to see if any ships were coming in to pick us up but no luck. Everyone was concerned with chasing down Jap ships or going to China for the battles there. I dreamt of home almost every night. Linc would not admit it but he was getting sicker by the day also. Brownie was just as bad. I feared that we might never get off this dammed island.

Chapter 5

The First Typhoon from Hell Sept 9, 1945

Toward the beginning of the second week of September around the 8th, I believe, the typhoon warning was issued for Okinawa. Several ships on the way to Tokyo would have to anchor in the Nahu harbor for protection from the storm. They had to ride it out in the harbor to prevent taking on water at sea. When the typhoon did actually hit on Sept 15 several ships broke loose, and were cast up on the beaches hundreds of yards from the ocean and had to be dug out and towed with tanks and cranes.

We headed for the caves on Sept 12 at around 08:00 in a truck convoy of supplies, and refugees by the hundreds. We also managed to secure some sleeping gear with us, and our sea bags. It was a long drive to the caves that lie to the south of Nahu. The Okinawan civilians had already been moved in big transport trucks with the Army MPs to large caves nearby found in the ridges that ran along the shore line on the west of the island. More caves are available on the eastern side of the island but the ride across the island over the coral ridges was too rough and dangerous by truck or jeep. We got to the cave none to soon as the winds and rain began to build up in intensity. It was as if the gods had turned on the 'faucet of the sky," and the winds and water that just came down harder and harder. The howling wind sounded like the roar of the thousands of dead soldiers that had died on this island coming back to life out of their anguish. Hell it was, and a wet hell at that. I had never experienced this destructive force of nature. A typhoon was truly nature at its worst. Nothing stood still in the wind of the typhoon. Everything took flight. Palm trees bent over to the ground in the high winds and the water gushed down the ridges washing everything into the valleys and flatlands below.

View of destruction from a destroyed building

The caves were large, damp, musty smelling and cold. The Army GIs made several fires to try to warm themselves and to provide something to cook on. The warmth from the fires was welcome. Getting dry wood was another problem we had not anticipated. Often we had to burn supply crates that were no longer needed. Pine crate wood is a soft wood and burns very fast. It was very difficult finding hardwood that would burn longer. Palm trees made a poor burning fuel. We were soaked to the skin even with rain ponchos on when we had to go out and search for more wood to keep the fires going. Radio contact with any ships was not possible and we went yet more days without hope of being picked up and taken back to Hawaii. "Brownie did you get any dry wood," I asked. "No, Chief, everything is wet. Maybe it will dry out if we keep it covered. Some of the GIs are using gasoline to start their fires because the wood is wet," Brownie commented. "Well I used a candle and it worked fine," I said. "Linc do you have any paper we can burn in your sea bag?" I asked. "No Chief, I don't even have a magazine or newspaper. I threw them out not thinking we would ever need paper when I was on the ship," said Linc. There was a fury of activity around us with the 10th Army moving crates into the caves and stacking them under tarps. We were like an island in the midst of the ocean that everyone had forgotten about. Being navy guys the Army usually ignored us. It was a sad state of affairs.

An Okinawan tornado moving in to decimate the island

The wind outside whistled through the cave causing all kinds of strange ghost-like sounds. The wind was so strong that it blew anything away that wasn't weighed down with rocks. Even hats could not stay on your head. The skies were dark day and night and the rain continued as if it were the monsoon season in India. The howling of the wind sounded like the dead crying out to the gods for help. Even playing poker was hard since if you put the cards down they blew away. The winds went from 50 mph up to 150 mph gusts. It had the rain traveling horizontally most of the time. You could not walk out in the exposed weather without being blown away and smashed into a rock mountain or tree stump.

We played cards a lot and poker was my specialty. Brownie, Linc, and I won a lot of food from the Army guys thanks to my poker playing ability and theirs. I taught Sam-boy how to play poker and he often sat and watched the games. "Sam boy what card is this, I said. I held up a 10 of spades and waited for Sam boy's response. "ohhh Ken san, one, two, four, nine, ten, black boy card, he said. We laughed and I said, "ten, ten of spades, Sam Boy, spades, little spades." Back in the old days on board the Antietam I made enough money at cards to be able to send some home. My natural poker face helped a lot and I had a photographic mind when it came to remembering what cards were played out and what weren't. My grandmother Ida Seabury taught me as a kid how to play Gin rummy, and Old-fashioned rummy and how to remember the cards played out. She could not read or write and came from a family of 13 children in Peekskill, New York, but she could play poker or rummy like a pro. Grandpa Nathaniel Seabury never beat her in rummy, despite his educated background (at the Peekskill Military Academy). He joined the Peekskill Police department in 1900 and later became the second Police Chief in the history of the city.

When I was a kid my parents would drop me and my brother Nate and sister Madeline off at Lake Oskawana, Putnam Valley for the entire summer. Every summer my grandparents brought us up to the lake. Grandpa Seabury was forced to retired in 1916 after 16 years as the Police Chief. He was a Republican and a new Democratic Mayor wanted to appoint his own Police Chief but the civil service rules prevented the Mayor from just firing him. So, the Mayor made up a series of false stories, paid some dubious characters to lie, and brought Chief Nathaniel Newcomb Seabury up on charges. Grandpa Seabury being an extremely honest man never saw it coming and thought that after his story was heard he would win. Unfortunately, the Mayor had a lot of paid liars, and Grandpa Seabury was forced to retire. He worked as a Security Guard at the hat factory in Buchanan, New York afterward and as a detective for a company in Bridgeport, Connecticut, over an hour away. Anyway, him and Grandma were avid card players and as a child, I got to watch and play cards with them every night for many, many summers. My poker playing ability really came in handy in the military service with the long hours of inactivity when not on duty. I had packed two decks of cards in my duffel bag, and that week of rain and wind, during the typhoon I became "food wealthy." Captain Tillen, and Sergeant "Wild Bill" Stanton challenged me to some poker several times, and I always won. Usually the officers played only officers but because I was a Navy Chief E-7, they treated me like a regular officer. There was nothing we could do during the typhoon except hunker down and wait. The roads were washed out. And the sea rose so high it completely washed away the beach area where we once had an encampment. Trees bent over and snapped and it was like the full-scale fury of hell had broken loose on the island. The winds were as high 140 mph and were tearing the tops of trees off, sending tents flying into the air along with Quonset huts.

I had thought that the hurricanes I had seen at Floyd Bennett field in New York were bad, but they were baby storms compared to a typhoon. Radio transmission continued to be down for the entire week. It was beginning to look pretty dismal with the weather conditions and the war being over and the priorities had changed to occupying Japan and its major cities and harbors as well as keep track of the problems with the Soviets invading Manchuria. I kept wondering if I have stayed on the Antietam just a little longer whether I would have done better than getting off on Okinawa. Sam-boy went out and brought back tropical fruits, bananas and green coconuts for the Army GIs and us. It was dangerous going out in the storm and I begged him not to go, but Sam boy had a mind of his own. He snuck out when I wasn't looking.

He was a very helpful little guy. We gave him some old Navy clothes we had as extras. Believe me there were wasn't extra clothing that fit us. Our regular clothing was rotting on our bodies because we only had a few uniforms each. I felt dirty and grimy all the time. We had to cut the pant legs short for Sam-boy to wear them, and the Navy shirt was so long we had to knot the shirt tails together and cut off the sleeves to short sleeve length. An upside down sailor cap sat on his head and with his bare feet he thought he was the greatest looking kid on the island. Thousands of other children, women and old men hid in the forests, and up on the Ryukyu ridge that stretched down the middle of the island. It was an elevated and steep ridge covered with tropical vegetation so thick you could not see someone hiding under a bush right in front of you. Most of the Okinawan men were dead from the war, and the only survivors were young children, women and old men. The Japanese conscripted thousands of able-bodied Okinawans to help them defend the island and most all them died doing that or were shot escaping or committed suicide by jumping off the coral cliffs.

The typhoon raged on and on during that week in Sept. 15-17, 1945. We did finally get some radio signals that the Antietam would be returning soon from the Yellow Sea to avoid any more typhoons, refuel in the bay and then return to the Yellow Sea again. I was saddened at the thought of the Antietam coming back but not being able to go onboard or return to Hawaii. My thoughts turned to survival. My gum disease had spread, and I had to take pain pills often. I woke up and two teeth were hanging by a thread from my gums. I pulled them out so I didn't choke on them. My feet had a permanent greenish mold on them that I could not wash away. The dampness was sinking into my bones like a sponge. I had started to grow a mustache when we first came ashore and now it was a full handlebar mustache. The biggest mustache I had ever grown, and that was because I never felt like or had time to trim it properly. Brownie and I were constantly sick. Each day was a struggle to go on. Lincoln had a skin rash like the one I had and Brownie complained about losing hair and having trouble with his fingernails. We had contracted a variety of unknown jungle diseases but could do nothing about it except keep taking medicine, which didn't work.

10th Army radioman, Okinawa 1945

We had a real surprise when we heard on the radio that Antietam would be returning to Okinawa on Sept. 13 to ride out the impending Typhoon in Nahu bay. We were looking forward to seeing some of our old ship hands. It was on all our minds to return to the Antietam and forget our original plans but we knew it was too late for that since we had all been replaced on the ship and it wasn't likely that the Captain would reverse his previous orders.

Early on Sept. 13th of September the Antietam came back into Nahu Bay. She was seeking shelter from in the small harbor from an impending typhoon. I was on the beach with Lincoln that morning, and Brownie was back in the headquarters compound not feeling well. It was the strangest feeling to be looking through binoculars, and see the Antietam with several destroyer escorts sailing over the horizon. In a matter of an hour or so she was anchoring in the harbor. Several re-supply boats were sent ashore to stock up on supplies for the ship. All the supplies were stockpiled at Kadema air base. This stockpiling was when the assault plans against Japan's mainland were still being considered back in July 1945, before the bombing of Japan.

(Japanese prisoners after the war in stockades, Okinawa 1945)

As it turned out we did not get to see anyone we knew until the typhoon was over on Sept. 21. The crew was given passes to go ashore for some liberty on Sept 22, 1945. The many days of being tossed around on a ship in a full-scale typhoon had made a lot of sailors sick. A big beer party was being planned to take everyone's mind off the terrible weeklong typhoon. We were able to talk with the Antietam's radioman several times and leave messages for some of our friends onboard that we were still on the island waiting to be picked up. The Executive office J.C. Alderman told us in a radio message that a destroyer would be picking us up within a week and he apologized for the Navy overlooking us on Okinawa. Finally there seemed to be hope that we would finally return home.

The beer party started around 15:00 hours, and continued until 23:00, when all sailors were due back on the Antietam. The beer party was a wild bash with beer keg after beer keg being popped open, and consumed as if there was no tomorrow. The kegs were stacked up neatly but left on the edge of the beach as the Antietam left at 06:30 the following day. We met all our old buddies and drank and drank all night long singing songs, telling stories and having a great time. The Executive officer J.C. Alderman, gave strict orders that the sailors were to have no contact with any of the Okinawans as suggested by the Army officers on shore. The MP security in the Okinawan stockade was heightened that evening to make sure there was no incident between any Okinawan women and the Antietam sailors. Still, everyone was happy to be on solid ground after being tossed around in his or her sleeping hammocks and mess hall for days. Many of the guys told us how after several days few sailors or officers could hold down any food at all. We were just happy to see someone we knew and shared the last year with during the war. By sunrise the next day they would be off again to the Yellow Sea to keep track of hostilities in China. We heard the U.S.S. Intrepid would also be anchored in the Yellow Sea with the Antietam.

The next morning the Antietam sailed off over the horizon and none of the three of us ever saw the ship leave since we all slept late due to all the drinking we did the night before. It was as if they came out of a dream and faded back into another dream when they left our lives. It would be the last time I would ever see the Antietam again.

October was approaching, and the weather would be changing soon, and getting cooler. Okinawa did not experience winters like Japan, and had a milder climate with year-round average temperatures of 60 degrees in the winter months, and 100 plus hot and humid temperature in the summer season. The temperature began to drop at nights and the dampness was always around us. Soon after the typhoon was over so we moved out of the cave back to a command headquarters new base further inland. Almost all of the tents and Quonset huts were destroyed during the typhoon so the Army command decided to seek better shelter further away from the beach area. Obviously, the Army had to figure a better method of anchoring the shelters and tents from being destroyed by typhoons.

Chapter 6

The Road to Shuri Castle

Captain Tillen got orders to check out the Shuri Castle, as it was called, on the Shuri battle scarred ridge. This high point was located inland from Nahu. It was here were so many American Marines and Army soldiers lost their lives trying to capture the Japanese headquarters. The Japanese officers had stationed themselves in the Shuri Temple that had a 2-4 foot thick stonewalls and gates surrounding it. The operative word was it had a 2-4 thick stonewall. The naval bombardment had flattened the entire palace and temple to a pile of rubble on a concrete platform. This 11th century temple-like palace sat at the highest point on Shuri ridge overlooking the island's bays and beaches.

There were reports that all the many caves near and around the Shuri castle were not fully closed off yet, and some Jap soldiers were still hiding in them. The June-July 1945 mop-up operation had done a pretty good job of fire torching all the caves, and either blowing them up or closing up the entrances. Tanks equipped with flamethrowers torched all the accessible caves, and most all of the caves on the island were dynamited closed by the Army and Marines.

The dispatch from headquarters was to double check these caves, and report back that they had all been searched, and destroyed to the last cave and tunnel. Night raids by Japs were still going on, especially near the Shuri castle and ridge. I didn't like caves or tunnels, but I went along since it would guarantee me some food, which I had completely run out of. Lincoln and Brownie were interested in collecting souvenirs so they decided to come along even though it could be dangerous. I had heard so many stories about the Shuri Castle that Lt. General Ushijima of the 32nd Japanese Army had commanded the defense of Okinawa from the heavily fortified 11th century complex. Huge stonewalls surrounded the castle making defense easy for the Japanese. An unobstructed view of the harbors from this elevated site helped the Japanese easily monitor the American landings. According to U.S. Army sources the castle was over 60,000 square meters (71,754 square yards) before the battle. The spectacular Shurei-mon (the second gate) stood at the castle as practically a national symbol of Okinawa. The first gate along the road to the Shuri castle was called "Ue No Torii (the upper gate) and the main huge stone gate along the road was called "Shita no tori" (the main gate). I got all that information from the U.S. Army historian.

The radio operator, Skip, said there were no American ships in the area and all the concentration was at the fleet in the China Sea. Other ships had returned to Hawaii without stopping by Okinawa. My gums were bleeding worse than ever and the skin rash I picked up from the dampness and lack of shower facilities was spreading from my hands up my arms. All I could put on my hands was hand lotion, and wash my hands many times a day. Nothing seemed to work. My clothes were beginning to rot and the stench was really getting to me. As I awoke that morning I was told we were having a meeting regarding some reports on Jap activity in and around the Shuri temple high up on the ridge.

Captain Brennerman asked me if I wanted to go with his division up to the Shuri Castle or stay near the Nahu beaches and the refugee tent city that was growing daily by hundreds of refugees. I did not like the idea of just staying around the refugee Okinawans, so the choice seemed to be the Shuri Castle or waste away on the beaches. At least I had some function as an interpreter since I had taught myself some Japanese expressions from Sam-boy, and could understand more and more of what the locals were saying. I left Sam-boy back in the refugee camp because this mission was too dangerous for him to come along. It was hard to believe that three months after the island of Okinawa was considered secured that Jap soldiers were still hiding out in caves all over the island. They were told by their officers never to surrender and that the honor of their families, and the Emperor were at stake. Several U.S. Army patrols in the Shuri area had reported sniper fire and nighttime shooting by some Jap soldiers who were coming out of their caves in search of food under cover of darkness. Since we were to the north of Shuri Castle it was going to be a long trip by jeep and walking to get up the ridge to the destroyed fortress. After the typhoon the roads were sure to be washed out, muddy, and difficult to drive a jeep over.

The Shuri Castle, now in ruins, had miles of caves under it and on surrounding hills. The U.S. Naval bombardments had shelled the Shuri ridge from the sea and flattened it to a pile of rubble with 45,000 shells. The once magnificent 11th-century Chinese Temple and surrounding walls and gates were now just a flat platform with assorted rocks and cracked pilings. The Japanese officers used the Shuri Castle as the command headquarters until the U.S. Marines and Army destroyed the entire compound with grenades, mortars and naval bombardment.

We left around 10:00 that following morning since it was expected to take most of the day climbing up the road that went up the long steep ridge that led to Shuri. The plan was to seek out the Jap soldiers at night and basically hunt them down like deer. Many of the Jap soldiers did not know the war was over and did not believe the reports they heard from the Okinawans. They thought it was all a plot to deceive them. It was a sad state of affairs when we had to have three GIs carry flame-thrower backpacks so we could torch them out of deep caves that were not safe to enter. It was an overcast day as we pulled out and headed for Shuri.

We heard that the Shuri Castle grounds miles of caves underneath spreading in all directions. Spent and also unexploded shells were supposed to be everywhere so we were cautioned to stay away from any shells. It would be a job trying to explode any shells that did not explode and were sticking in the mud like duds. I caught a ride on the back of a jeep and we bounced and swayed all the way up the rut filled path which was supposed to be a main road to Shuri. All I could think of was when was the Navy going to get that destroyer to pick us up and was the Antietam Executive Officer talking seriously about someone coming soon to pick us up? I guess three sailors trapped on an island was low priority in relation to all the other problems being faced by the Navy during the month of September 1945, but three men should make some difference.

We passed many shallow graves along the side of the road. Skulls, bones from all parts of the body were strewn everywhere in the mud. It was like a plane had flown overhead and dumped out tons of dried body parts and bones. It was truly a garden of bones. Many decaying forms that were once humans lay along the side of the road with teeming maggots all over them. You never get used to the signs of death and death itself. The stench of death was everywhere. There was an acid smell with flies, and bugs flying around as if we were driving up a huge mountain size dung heap.

I could see that many of the rice paddies and sweet potato fields were bombed out, with no water or plants due to dried out bomb holes. The fields looked like someone had tried to plant vegetation on the moon. We crossed over many shallow rivers running downhill from the ridges that seemed to dominate the entire island. As far as the eye could see were the coral ridges running from the east coast to the west coast of Okinawa covered in a blanket of green foliage.

It was about midday when we took a break to look for some local food and open up our K-rations. All I had left was a can of beans that I had won in a poker game. Linc and Brownie didn't fare much better with food. I decided to get some spring water for our canteens and went down to a mountain stream nearby.

We had just stopped to rest when two old women came along dragging what looking like their life's possessions piled several feet in the air behind them on a small handcart made of wooden wheels. They were struggling to pull the heavy two-wheeled cart down the muddy road. As they approached, one of the GIs yelled, "halt" in English, then again in Japanese. They continued to come closer as if to go around us when suddenly there was a huge explosion sending a cloud of black smoke in all directions and metal shrapnel, wood splinters and rocks shot out in all directions killing the old women and blowing up one of our jeeps. Gasoline spread everywhere and the entire area was aflame in black smoke and the smell of burnt rubber as the tires burned down to lumps of black goo. There was screaming and yelling everywhere. Linc and Brownie were taking a leak off the side of the road and when the explosion hit they dropped to the ground covering their head and rocks and flying metal hit them in their helmets. Lucky for them they were wearing their helmets the Army had given them for safety. Linc got nicked in the arm from shrapnel and was bleeding profusely. Brownie took a handkerchief out of his back pocket and wrapped it around Linc's arm.

Sadly, and without warning two GIs, Pfc. Gary Smoltz and Pfc. Ted Danner were killed by the blast instantly since they were leaning against the jeep at the time of the explosion. The Sarg was bellowing orders and telling the troops to drop to the ground. Chaos and confusion was everywhere. Then as suddenly as the noise came it went with one of the jeeps in flames. We had no way of putting out the fire, so we had to push on before the ammunition in the jeep exploded too.

I ran back when I heard the explosion when I was down by the stream a 100 yards away filling my canteen. "Brownie, you OK!" I called out. "Linc, where are you," I yelled. "Down here Chief," they responded. I ran over to the side of the road fully expecting them to be injured. Fortunately, Linc was ok with his bleeding and Brownie taking care of him. "Thank God you guys are alright," "Linc are you OK?" I said. We knew from then on that this would be no picnic and no one could be trusted.

Sergeant Stanton radioed for a jeep to take the bodies back to the base and we put Linc on the jeep to go back to get better attention to his wound. Cursing aloud the terrors of war, we learned to trust no one from that point on. Captain Tillen was back at the command center giving orders to shoot first, and ask questions afterward if any civilian or Jap solder attempted to approach. We had to stay there for about an hour until another jeep arrived, and we were able to gather up the remains of the two soldiers and wrap them in canvas. We were forced to double up on riders in the remaining jeeps. Unfortunately, Linc had to return to the base with his injury. We had a one half-track truck full of supplies, ammunition and explosives in a vehicle that could climb anywhere.

By 1700 hours we reached the plateau that was once the Shuri Temple. The view was magnificent from this vantage point and it was easy to see why the Jap officers had chosen it. We searched the area the rest of the day for caves and marked them on our roughly drawn map. The plan was to place some land mines near the openings of some of the caves and some cans on strings to make noise at night so we could tell if someone was coming out of the hundreds of large and small caves all around the ridge. Some of the large cave openings had already been blocked by boulders and from mortar shells that destroyed the openings to the caves.

It was going to be a full moon that night providing plenty of light to see any Jap soldiers coming out of their caves. A 50mm machine gun was put in place on the edge of the ridge that had a perfect view of dozens of cave openings along the side of the ridge. The flamethrower would go out with different patrols that night to torch out any Japs. This was going to be a difficult and dangerous operation. I practiced Japanese expressions like the "konnichiwa, Ohayou, arigatou, O-namae wo oshie-te kudasai, Eigo wo hanashi-masu-kaWatashi wa jouzu-ni nihongo ga hanase masen, Eigo wo hanasu hiti wa imasen-ka." Needless to say I was scared stiff, and so was Brownie. We had never hunted in the dark before except at my grandfather's house on Lake Oscawana in Putnam Valley, just 20 miles outside of Peekskill, New York. We used to go coon hunting at night with single shot rifles. Grandpa was more interested in scaring the raccoons than actually killing them. They were a menace to garbage cans and caused a lot of damage trying to break into outdoor toolboxes to eating the glue on newly made canoes.

Night came fast, and we smothered the fires and waited along various vantage points for movement in the brushes. Eventually around 23:00 a Jap soldier stuck his head out from behind a rock and the moonlight reflected off his face for a moment. A barrage of bullets from a GI's machine gun and other GI guns let loose at the same time. It looked like the Fourth of July on Shuri ridge that night. The sky lit up with hundreds of bullets aimed in the direction of one Jap soldier who did not know that dozens of guns were trained on his position. The Jap soldier never had a chance at least a hundred bullets must have riddled his body. The noise scared any other Jap soldiers and that was the only one we found that evening.

The next day after resting from an all night vigil we moved out to find caves in daylight and torch the Japs out if we could not talk them into surrendering. My nerves were starting to act up and my hand was trembling like a shaking leaf in the wind. Brownie was having second thoughts about getting souvenirs we took two flame-throwers with our patrol and headed down a narrow and very steep trail off the side of the remains of the Shuri Castle. The trail was difficult to descend with a rifle in one arm and a pack with ammunition in the other hand. I slipped several times when rocks under my feet washed out. The first cave we came to had evidence of a recent fire at the entrance. We called into the cave in Japanese to come out, "Hello, and konnichiwa." There was no response. We repeated it several times until the Master Sargent gave the order to blow them up. One of the GIs threw in a grenade and the whole cave wall collapsed. We heard nothing so we moved onto another cave that was a little wider. I threw a rock into the cave and called out in Japanese to "konnichiwa."

There was no response. I repeated "konnichiwa," several more times. Then without any warning a gun went off inside the cave ricocheting off the cave walls. Sargent Stanton called out to the GI with the flamethrower to let it rip. A huge flame 20-30 feet long shot into the cave and screams came out but no one left the cave. Since it was too dangerous to enter the cave with all the boulders blocking full view we threw in two grenades and waited. No one came out so two GIs were sent in to check the results. Three Jap soldiers and two civilian women were dead at the back of the cave.

We moved onto the next cave right off the side of a steep cliff. The same routine went on all day long, grenade or flamethrower and blast the cave closed at the end. Not one Jap soldier surrendered the entire day. At best I can remember we killed 48 Jap soldiers, and 15 civilians that day and took no one prisoner.

The next night we strung up cans on wire to let us know if any Japs were trying to get inside our perimeter. It was pitch black that night and no moon was out. Sure enough around 4:00 in the morning the cans began to jingle. Everyone let loose with a volley of bullets. We could not see what we hit but the cans stopped making noise. The following morning we went to inspect how many Japs we had killed. There on the wire dead from hundreds of bullets was a stray goat. Needless to say we dragged the goat back to the camp and had roasted goat for lunch that day.

After the three-day cleanup operations we would be returning to the beach headquarters at Nahu. I missed Linc and hoped he was OK with that shoulder wound. Good news finally came in a radio dispatch sent to the command center and passed on to us. The radioman said the Navy had indicated that a "tin can" or destroyer was cleared to anchor in the harbor and pick all three of us up in the next two or three days. It was in the China Sea area and got the message form the Executive Officer J.C. Alderman of the Antietam to pick us up on its way back to Hawaii for some repairs and refueling. Finally, there seemed to be a light at the end of the tunnel. Brownie, and I slapped one another's hands and were so thrilled we could hardly sleep that night.

Back at the Headquarters I awoke the next morning with a giant spider walking down my arm. I cursed and swatted it off. Lincoln was still recovering from his shoulder wound. He had a mess of cockroaches the size of rats under his bunk eating a cracker that had fallen out of his pants. They were huge and ugly like in a science fiction movie. I grabbed my shoe and crushed them all with several well-aimed thrusts. The wind was picking up that day and the trees were bending under another impending storm. The clouds overhead was beginning to gather. I felt like crap again. My skin problem was bothering me and several of my teeth just fell out when I was chewing on a dried piece of meat. I knew then I had contracted some kind of jungle disease that was affecting my skin and gums. The only thing the medic could give me was a painkiller, which really did not help.

Daily survival was becoming a major task. The three day patrol to Shuri ridge had tired Brownie and I out completely. Linc was lucky he wasn't killed by the exploding wagon. I hadn't see Sam Boy for several days. He appeared that morning with some fresh bananas he has picked from a tree. We thanked him for the fresh fruit. I played a game of poker with Sam Boy and let him win easily. He got a kick out of repeating "Ken san," as he called me. When would that destroyer be docking in Nahu bay, I asked myself. It was difficult being patient. I was feeling depressed and sick from sore gums and skin rashes on my left arm.

Chapter 7

Revisit to Sugar Loaf Hill

A view of Sugar Loaf Hill long after the battle in the spring of 1945

Another patrol was being organized to look for Japs hiding in Nahu and in Okinawan tombs nearby. I volunteered just to have something to do. Brownie stayed behind with Linc and Sam Boy. We passed more Okinawan civilians on the way Nahu and gave them a wide berth from out previous problem with the old women with the wooden cart. On the way to the Nahu ruins we went past several hills, which I was told, had a unique history. 150 yards south of Uchitomari ridge, and the Nishi Baru Ridge, and the village of Kakazu, lies near a small hill (50 feet high and 300 yards long) named by the invading American troops "Sugar Loaf Hill." The U.S. Army historian could never stop talking about this hill. He told me the name was given by the Americans who fought so bravely to break through the Japanese Shuri line of defenses that dreaded spring of 1945. It was a hill that was captured, and lost 11 times leaving causalities in the thousands for the Americans. It was in the crossfire of Jap troops that had the protection of caves and elevation with a perfect view of the gateway hill called "Sugar Loaf Hill." The Japanese artillery fire was deadly accurate and caused many casualties for the American troops. What made the Japanese artillery so accurate was the fact that this area was actually their artillery training ground and they knew the terrain extremely well.

Okinawan civilians 1945

I looked at the tree bald hill and could not understand why it cost us so many lives. Sugar Loaf hill was part of a complex of three hills and was the western anchor of General Mitsuru Ushijiam' Shuri line of defense that ran from coast to coast across the island of Okinawa. I could see the ridges behind Sugar Loaf hill and they had a perfect view of the hill.

I learned the battle for Sugar Loaf hill began on May 12, and lasted until May 18, 1945. Two days later the Japanese made a surprise counter-attack of battalion size and failed thanks to the valor of the U.S. troops defending the captured hill. I could see Sugar Loaf Hill over the flat farmlands from the harbor at Nahu and it is a significant topographical feature on the island. In seven days of fighting the 6th U.S. Marine division took 2,000 casualties. Now it was a bald stump of a hill with no trees left on it. Shell holes were everywhere like the craters on the moon. It did not look very impressive, but it sat in the middle between several ridges on the way up to the Shuri castle and the headquarters of the Japanese army. We searched every Okinawan tomb and ruins of homes and found not Japs hiding. It was a most uneventful day.

When we returned to the beach command post north of Nahu that afternoon, around 13:00 hours, the Okinawan refugee tent camp had grown three times larger than it was before we left. Hunger was everywhere and starvation was seen in the eyes of all the civilians. A huge temporary feeding facility was set up for the Okinawans to eat at while in the refugee compound. Now the GI cooks had enlisted the support of dozens of Okinawan Camp women who helped with cooking at the refugee detainment camp.

(Okinawan women who helped in the camps with food serving and cooking)

Okinawan woman were needed to prepare meals on a large-scale basis for the refugees were a major asset. Rice, and other foodstuffs were air dropped onto the beach every day to prevent the civilians and the U.S. Army from starving to death. This was the first time I didn't have to beg for food. Up to this point my poker playing ability kept the three of us alive with food I won. By U.S. Army orders we really did not exist. It was a hard learned lesson for us. I think I lost about 10 pounds, and so did Linc and Brownie. Our health was declining daily and there seemed to be little we could do about it. Seeing the Shuri ruins, and Sugar Loaf Hill were memorable sites I will never forget. I dreamt about being shelled every night in my dreams. It was difficult falling asleep at night with so much destruction on my mind. The heat, humidity were constant reminders of a living hell on earth. I could not wait for that Destroyer to arrive and get out of this hell.

Chapter 8

The Second Typhoon—Oct. 9, 1945

October was approaching in two days, and the radio operator did not hear from the Destroyer operating in the China Sea. Another warning came through that a typhoon was forming off the Caroline Islands and could hit Okinawa on October 8, 1945. We again had to drop all the tents, and get the trucks together and flee for the caves. This time the number of Okinawan refugees had doubled, so that was a major problem in moving them in available trucks again to the southern caves. Chaos was rampant as the Okinawans could sense the urgency of the U.S. Army to protect them and all of the soldiers on the island.

Typhoon damage on Okinawa 1945

On the evening of October 8, the storm began to slow down before hitting Okinawa. This was only a brief pause as it began to greatly increase in intensity. The sudden shift of the storm caught many ships by surprise, small craft in the constricted waters of Nahu Bay, and they were unable to escape to sea. I guess they were hoping the typhoon would veer out to sea and not hit Okinawa. Whatever their reasoning they had plenty of time to prepare and chose not to do so. Brownie, Linc, and I packed our stuff and put it on a truck headed to the caves. I sent Sam Boy back to the civilian stockade where he would be safer. We had gone through this process before and had great fear of these typhoons.

On October 9th, the typhoon hit the island with winds of 80 knots (92 miles per hour) and 30-35 foot waves battered the ships and craft in the Bay. The Army's tents, Quonset huts and buildings ashore were all starting to blow away. We did not have enough time to take down all the tents.

Damage to many ships after the typhoon was extensive in 1945

Here is an extract on the typhoon from Commander in Chief, Pacific Fleet and Pacific Ocean Areas—Typhoon "Louise," 9 October 1945 Storm at Okinawa.

> "On 4 October a typhoon developed just north of Rota as a result of a barometric depression and the convergent flow of equatorial air and tropical air. Guam Weather Central called the storm of apparently weak intensity "Louise" and put out the first weather advisory on

it at 041200Z, with further advisories following at intervals of six hours. Up to that time of the 16th advisory (080600Z), the storm was following a fairly predictable path to the NW, and was expected to pass between Formosa and Okinawa and on into the East China Sea. At this time, however, the storm began to veer sharply to the right and head north for Okinawa. The 17th advisory at 081200Z (081100I) showed this clearly, and units began to be alerted for the storm late in the evening of the 8th. The forecast for Okinawa was for winds of 60 knots, with 90-knot gusts in the early morning of 9 October, and passage of the center at 1030(I). "Louise", however, failed to conform to pattern, and that evening, as it reached 25° N (directly south of Okinawa) it slowed to six knots and greatly increased in intensity." (Commander in Chief, Pacific Fleet)

The storm that struck in the afternoon of the Oct. 9th and came on suddenly very strong. The September typhoon did not match this typhoon in fury and violence. It was becoming the worst storm at Okinawa since the Allied landings in April 1945. According to the radio operator the storm took a sudden shift of the 12 hours before. Many craft in the supposedly safe shelter of Nahu Bay were surprised by the sudden change in direction of the typhoon.

On the ninth of October Nahu Bay was jammed with ships ranging in size from Victory ships to LCVs. All units, both afloat and ashore, were hurriedly battening down and secured for the storm. The U.S. Army had it's own problems moving Jap prisoners, Okinawan civilians and all of the 10th U.S. Army to caves for shelter from the typhoon.

While we were driving back and forth to the caves the wind speed picked up causing the canvas on the large transport trucks to rip off. Civilians in the back of the trucks were at the mercy of the winds and salt spray. The beaches were washing away and the tops of trees near the beaches were bring ripped right off. Brownie, Linc and I could not see more than a few hundred yards with the wind, sand and rain coming down. By 1200, visibility was zero, and the wind was 60 knots from the east and northeast, with tremendous seas breaking over the ships. Small craft were already being torn loose from their anchors, and larger ships were, with difficulty, holding by liberal use of their engines. We watched from the caves when a few boats tore lose of their anchors and washed ashore on the island during the storm.

At 1400 the wind had raised to 80 knots, with gusts of far greater intensity, the rain that drove in horizontally was more salt than fresh, and even the large ships were dragging anchor under the pounding of 30 to 35-foot seas. We could not even see some of the ships because the waves were washing over the decks.

Nahu bay was now in almost total darkness, and we could not see any of the ships anchored. The scene was one of utter confusion as ships suddenly loomed in the darkness, collided, or barely escaped colliding by skillful use of engines, and was as quickly separated by the heavy seas. Not all ships were lucky; hundreds were blown ashore, and frequently several were cast on the beach in one general mass of wreckage, while the crews worked desperately to maintain watertight integrity and to fasten a line to anything at hand in order to stop pounding.

Many ships had to be abandoned. Sometimes other ships took aboard the crews; more often they made their way ashore, where they spent a miserable night huddled in caves and fields. A few were lost. There was nothing we could do on land but watch and listen over the radio. Thank God we were on land because everyone at sea was in great peril. The Okinawan civilians were crying and their voices seem to float above the sound of the wind. The caves only made the sounds worse by echoing back and forth. It was a most unnerving sound.

By 1600 hours the winds got worse, and the typhoon reached its peak, with steady winds of 100 knots and frequent gusts of 120 knots. We had several wind instruments we brought with us to keep track of how bad the storm was. The wind speed detector was attached to one of the jeeps and it was spinning so fast I thought it would take off into the air.

I had been on a ship in 20-knot winds and that was a gale storm, but 100 knots was unbelievable. At this time the barometer dipped to 968.5 millibars. The radio operator kept getting a lot of information over the airways as many ships were calling for help. This was the lowest reading that the barometers recorded, and was probably the point of passage of the center of the typhoon, but the maximum winds continued unabated for another many hours, the gusts becoming fiercer, if anything. During this period, the wind shifted to the north, and then to the northwest, and began to blow ships back off the west and north reefs of the Bay and across to the south, sometimes dragging anchors the entire way. The ships were tossed around like little toys. These wild voyages by damaged ships caused a nightmare series of collisions and near escapes with other drifting ships and shattered hulks.

The radioman described a typical experience during the storm. A ship named FLAGLER was dragging her anchors dragged at noon, and despite the use of both engines she was blown ashore a mile north of the bay colliding with an LST on the way. Once grounded, she began to pound, and all power was lost. At 1710, as the wind changed, FLAGLER was blown off the reef and back across the bay, grazing a capsized YF and continuing on, with a 13° port list, no power, and the lower spaces and after engine room beginning to flood. One anchor was lost, the other dragged across the bay. The ships looked like corks bobbing around in a bottle. The rain was blowing horizontally and we could not see much in the harbor because of the fog and darkness in the sky.

Conditions on shore were no better especially in the caves. Water was running through the caves and dripping off the walls everywhere. There wasn't a dry spot in the caves anywhere. Brownie, Linc, and I used some crates to keep us dry and off the cave floor. By spreading a tarp over the supplies crates we were able to keep relatively dry as the water poured through the cave. We tried to play cards but the wind was so strong we could not put cards down without them blowing away. Fires in the cave provided some warmth but also fogged up the air with smoke making it difficult to see. We were playing a wait and see game. When necessary some of the caves were converted into temporary hospitals for the injured.

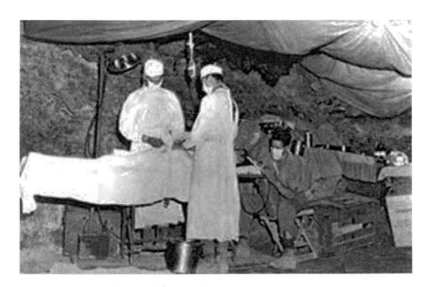

Temporary hospital set up in Okinawan caves 1945

Twenty hours of torrential rain soaked everything, made quagmires of roads, and eventually ruined all supplies in crates sitting on the beaches. We were unable to use the roads even with half-tracks because the mud was so deep. The hurricane winds destroyed from 50% to 95% of all tent camps, and flooded the remainder. Damage to Quonset huts ran from 40% to 99% total destruction. Some of these Quonsets were lifted bodily and moved hundreds of feet; others were torn apart, galvanized iron sheets ripped off, wall boarding shredded, and curved supports torn apart. Driven from their housing, officers and men alike were compelled to take shelter in caves with us. Old tombs, trenches, and ditches in the open fields were shelter for anyone caught in the storm. Even heavy road-building machinery was flipped over, as the wind swept tents, planks, and sections of galvanized iron through the air. "Brownie do you want a can of beans," I asked. "Thanks Chief," he said, "I have plenty of cans of beans." "How is Sam boy doing," I asked. "I am sure he is surviving as he always does Chief," Linc answered. "How long is this typhoon going to last?" I said. "Too long for me," Brownie commented.

I heard that at Kadema air base some 60 planes of all types were damaged, some of which had been tossed about unmercifully, but most of which were repairable. Installations suffered far more severely. The seas worked under many of the concrete ramps and broke them up into large and small pieces of rubble. All repair installations were either swept away or severely damaged. At Yonobaru up north, all 40' by 100' buildings were demolished. Communication and meteorological services were blown out at most bases by 1900. We were in a desperate situation.

Damage to Kadema air force base from the typhoon 1945

The storm center of typhoon "Louise" passed Nahu Bay at about 16:00, from which time until 20:00 it raged at peak strength. The storm was advancing at the rapid rate of 15 knots in a northerly, then northeasterly, direction, and by 20;00 the center was 60 miles away. The winds gradually began to subside. Conditions in Nahu Bay were at this time somewhat improved by the winds having veered to the northwest across the land mass of Okinawa, which reduced the size of the seas, and probably saved many more damaged ships from being driven off the reefs and sunk in deep water.

Compared to the typhoon we had in September this typhoon was like a "super-typhoon" with steady winds of 80 and 60 knots throughout the night, and some gusts of higher velocity. All hands spent a wild, wet, and dangerous night, afloat or ashore. It was not until 1000 on the next day that the winds fell to a steady 40 knots and rains slackened. It was still too early to head back to our headquarters site. I leaned over a small fire to get warm. "brrr it is cold and damp as hell in this cave," I said. I lost another tooth this morning with my jungle disease that was attacking my gums. Soon I would be gumming my food. There was no dental treatment available except rubbing whiskey on my gums.

By the third day typhoon "Louise", had left its damage it behind on Okinawa. Approximately 80% of all housing and buildings were destroyed or made unusable. Very little tentage was salvageable, and little was on hand as a result of previous storms. Food stocks were left for only 10 days. Medical facilities were so destroyed that an immediate request had to be made for a hospital ship to support the shore activities on the island. Casualties were low, considering the great numbers of people concerned and the extreme violence of the storm. This was very largely due to the active and well directed efforts of all hands in assisting one another, particularly in evacuation of grounded and sinking ships. "Brownie, Linc, wake up, I think I see the sun coming out," I said. It was the third day and finally there seemed to be a break in the weather. In the night two women were blown away by the winds and killed when they hit a rock wall.

By October 18, 1945, radio reports found that there were 36 dead and 47 missing, with approximately 100 injured. A total of 12 ships were sunk, 222 grounded, and 32 damaged beyond the ability of ships' companies to repair. We had several civilians swept away in the storm and several injuries to the Army from getting hit with flying objects.

Vice Admiral W. W. Smith inspected the damage, and decided that only 10 ships were worth complete salvage, out of some 90 ships with major work to be done on them. This decision was made chiefly because similar types of ships were rapidly being decommissioned in the United States, and the cost of salvage would have been excessive for unneeded ships.

Repair work went on rapidly ashore as of the fourth day after the typhoon. As a result of the experience in the earlier typhoon in September, extra stocks of food and tents were stored on Okinawa in the caves. Supplies were enroute on October 12, 1945, and in less than a week after the storm, supplies were fairly well built up; emergency mess halls and sleeping quarters were being erected for everyone. "Brownie give me a hand with that crate, I cannot lift it by myself," I said. We were heading into the fourth day and we were moving back to the U.S. Army Headquarters near Nahu bay. "Linc are you OK with the lifting?" I asked. ? "Sure Chief, I am hanging in there even though my back is killing me." "OK, just let Brownie and I know if you need a rest," I said. It was a tough day moving everything out of the caves and back on the trucks. The MPs had already loaded the Okinawan civilians on trucks early in the day and most of them had already been moved back to Nahu Bay.

It took over an hour to ride back to the U.S. Army headquarters. We arrives around 13:00 hours to see all the damage. Nothing was left of the compound or the headquarters. The Quonset huts blew away, the rolled up tents were gone and flooding was everywhere. We had to move to higher and dryer ground in order to put back up tents.

Smitty, Linc and I never worked so hard in our entire lives setting up thousands of tents and helping to build new huts. The heat and humidity was brutal during the day, and work progressed slowly both day and night. Brownie and I pitched in and helped put up tents and move supplies to more secured areas. It was so hot and humid I had a constant headache the whole time. My shirt was dripping in sweat and dirt. Linc could not lift anything because of his shoulder wound was still healing. "God, I cannot take this heat on Okinawa," I said. "It feels like an oven and we are the meat cooking inside," Brownie commented. At least the sun had returned and things were starting to dry out. We had to search around for another tent that wasn't ripped. The U.S. Army had its work cut out for it. The Okinawan civilians were helping build their own compound mostly to keep to Japanese soldiers from entering in the night. They were afraid of both the Japanese and the Americans. It was reported that some Japanese officers were hiding in the Okinawan compound but none had been discovered yet.

All of the U.S. Army on the island were engaged in attempting to recover from the typhoon damage. Boxes of food were found in open fields miles from the base. It was a giant mess, and a nightmare for the Okinawans in the stockades. Many of the Okinawan civilians pitched in and helped put up thousands of tents for their families. It took many over a week to recover. I lost track of where Sam boy was in all the excitement. I assumed he was with all the Okinawan civilians in the many caves.

In the midst of all the rebuilding activities one of the GIs stepped on a land mind and was blown to bits. We had a funeral service for him the next day. I still remember his name, Corporal Devers Greenland. It was hard to believe that land minds still existed. Sargent Stanton and anti-mine patrols stepped up in and around the stockades and the U.S. Army headquarters. A few mines were discovered and defused. I felt a lot better knowing that anti-personnel mines could be anywhere. It taught us to walk softly and on established paths, not on the side of the roads.

The nights were getting cooler now that the autumn air had moved in. Fortunately, the days warmed up fast after the chilling nights. All we had to sleep in were U.S. Army issued sleeping bags that were not that warm. Sam Boy came and went from our tent to the Okinawan stockade on a daily basis. He would get food from us and trade it in the Okinawan stockade. Already he was becoming a little businessman. "Sam boy how are you doing?" I asked. "OK, OK Ken san," he replied. "Do you want to play cards?" I asked. "Yes, yes, me Sam boy want play cards with you Ken san," he replied. He was beginning to understand how to play poker but had trouble naming the cards in English. Words like King or Queen were hard for him to say. Sometimes he would call them "kin san and quee san," which would make us all laugh. I had some Army chocolate I gave him that day and I was thrilled to taste something so sweet.

The hope of that Destroyer coming to pick us up was fading. We were beginning to feel that the message the Chief Executive Office got was a phony. I tried to put it out of my mind. I lost another tooth that morning from my jungle disease that was attacking my gums.

The rebuilding process went on all week day and night. The U.S. Army worked in shifts and used any able bodied Okinawans to help with cooking, and setting up the hundreds of pup tents for the Okinawans. The U.S. Army erected much larger tents for its own personnel that could house 6-8 soldiers each. It was a slow and muddy process with the heat and humidity to slow things down even more.

Chapter 9

Recovery from the Typhoon of Oct. 9, 1945

After the Typhoon the whole island looked like a mud graveyard. Everything was destroyed including the refugee camp, the Army tents, huts and temporary buildings. Boxes and equipment were found miles from their origin. Much of the stockpiles at the airport were scattered all over. It was amazing how much damage a 150 mph wind could do. The recovery progress was slow, and the refugees alone took many days to transport. Every truck on the island was in use helping to move supplies and recover from the typhoon. These winds were certainly no "Divine Winds,' as the Japanese called them. They only extended the suffering of the Okinawan people and the war captives.

This time the damage was even more severe than the Typhoon in Sept. 1945. We had several deaths this time involving Okinawan Civilians being thrown into the air or being hit by flying objects. The first aid tent had a line around the perimeter area of Okinawans and soldiers that had slight to severe injuries. Brownie, Linc and I were just happy to have survived yet another Typhoon without being injured.

We began to worry if any ship would come to rescue us with so many dangerous typhoons threatening the island. Still the radio transmission was completely out most of the time and in the process of being repaired. "Brownie did you check in with the radio operator today," I said. "Sure Chief about an hour ago I listened to some of the radio chatter in the radio shack, No work yet Chief," Brownie said. "What do you thing linc? Are we ever going to get off this dam island? I responded.

My jungle disease was causing me a lot of pain, and Linc was still recovering from his shrapnel wound. Brownie's only problem was his stomach acting up. Food supplies were beginning to pile up and we are able to secure more k-rations to help us get through the days. Sam Boy was still hanging around and had brought us some sweet potatoes he had found in a farm field. We cooked the sweet potatoes over a small fire until they were well cooked. It was a great treat after eating k-rations for so long.

The Army engineers had set about bringing in another Quonset hut and securing it to the same site the last headquarters was located. We had to put up our tent again which we had taken down and rolled up and tied to several boulders for safety.

Inside one of the Quonset huts on Okinawa 1945

The skies were beginning to clear and although everything was wet, it was beginning to look like things were going to improve. Hope was on the way. Sam Boy told us of the fear of the Okinawan civilians during the typhoon. Many of the women cried the entire three days during the storm. He said he hid under a box in one of the caves. I felt sorry for him and the rest of the refugees on the island. The fury of a typhoon was more than any of had ever seen in our lifetimes. "So you survived, yes Sam boy," I said to Sam boy. "Yes, Ken san, I live," he said. I talked about living back home in New York that day for about an hour or so and he listened and tried to understand. "Chief, we have to get back to work and round up some wood for a small fire tonight to dry out,"

Brownie said. "Where is Linc," I asked. "He is over at the first aid tent getting some medicine," Brownie responded. "I hope he is OK." I said. We were all sicker than ever before but we tried not to think about it. I had a headache practically everyday and stomach cramps too.

I could not imagine getting hit with typhoons every year during the summer and autumn months. Autumn winds to me brought the vision of leaves falling in New York and the many colors of trees in the fall. Autumn winds in New York were always gentle. The nights in New York were getting colder in autumn announcing the coming of winter in late November and early December. Here in Okinawa was the fear of typhoons could kill and blow peoples houses away.

My dreams at night ranged from sinking at sea in a ship, to being blown to pieces after stepping on an anti-personnel land mine. It was not easy trying to fall asleep. We have been on Okinawa for over a month and no ship to retrieve us had yet to show up.

Chapter 10

The Light at the end of the Tunnel

A soldier stuck his head in our tent and told us the radio operator had been in contact with the Battleship U.S.S. Idaho, which would be docking in Nahu bay sometime that day. We were told to meet a launch at the floating docks on the beach. We hurriedly starting putting our stuff in our sea bags. Finally there seemed to be hope of getting home.

U.S.S. Idaho Battleship, WWII, Okinawa 1945

The Battleship U.S.S. Idaho pulled into harbor at 09:00 on Oct. 20th, and sent a launch to pick us up at the Nahu beach. It was one of the best days of our lives. Our days as Okinawan Island survivors had finally come to an end after one-½ months of typhoons, sickness, Japanese snipers, and field mines. Sam boy was there to help us pack. He was sad we were leaving. We talked about America and where I lived in New York for a while. I gave him $20 U.S. money and a deck of cards, and told him to look me up someday if he ever came to America. He was so grateful he cried. I was Ken san, his adopted father on Okinawa and I was leaving him all alone, and without any family. It saddened me to leave him there but I had no choice. We were on the temporary docks waiting for the launch to come. Sam boy was there, Linc and Brownie. As the launch pulled up to the dock we tied it off and threw our sea-bags into the boat. I gave Sam boy a hug and said goodbye. We all waved to Sam boy as the launch moved our in to the harbor. It was the last time I would see Sam boy. I waved to Sam boy from the boat. He waved back.

The battleship Idaho was on the way back to Hawaii, and was loaded with soldiers, marines and sailors whose enlistments were up and were returning home. My bunk turned out to be a small corner of the deck space where I had to tie myself to a pipe so as not to roll away in the night. Even the mess galley was overcrowded, but the mood was light since the war was over, and we were finally returning home. The waves were splashing over the bow and the Battleship pounded through the waves and the mist hit me in the face every now and then but I did not care. I was free of Okinawa and on my way home. Linc and Brownie were strapped down to the deck next to me. The only time we got up was to go to the head or get some chow inside. It was so crowded inside that Sailors were standing because there was no place to sit. Everyone suffered through the crowded conditions because we were all happy to go home. I was eating some crackers when a wave splashed over the port side of the ship and washed the cracker right out of my hands. "Brownie, did you see that," I laughed. "The wave swept my cracker out of my hand," I said. "It is going to be a rough trip back Chief," Brownie said. "These tin cans were made for speed and battle not for comfort and the on-deck view was minimal," said Brownie. Linc was dozing off and not paying attention to our chatter. It would be only two days until we got to Hawaii and after all the suffering we went through on Okinawa this seemed like a picnic. "Thank God," I shouted out. Linc and Brownie looked at my like I had lost my mind.

On Oct. 22, 1945, a month after Brownie, Lincoln, and I stepped off on Okinawa, we had returned to Hawaii. After two days of R and R at Hawaii, I was off again on the battleship Idaho, to return to Virginia via the Panama Canal.

Oct. 29, 1945 I got a four-day pass to go ashore at Coco Solo, Panama Canal Zone. Panama was as hot as you can get with humidity so high that you sweat all the time. I ate everything in site since I had not eaten properly for over a month while stranded on Okinawa. My jungle disease on my hands still existed and most of my teeth had fallen out already from the ordeal on Okinawa.

The battleship Idaho arrived at Norfolk, Virginia on Oct. 31, 1945. Later that day, I received my final transfer papers, and was given permission to go ashore. I was to report to the processing center in Long Beach, Long Island, New York. I bought a train ticket and got on the train to return to Penn Station on 32nd Street between 7th and 8th Avenues in New York City. Carrying my canvas sea bag, which weighed a ton, I caught a subway to Basiley Park, Queens to finally see my bride of four years and my three-year-old son. I called my wife Doris from the pay phone and told her to expect me sometime around 6:00 that evening. She was thrilled and excited to hear from me since the mail delivery from the Pacific area since the treaty was unreliable.

As I got off the bus in Baisley Park, I had a one-block walk to where my wife was living with her mother in a small rented apartment on the second floor in a two family house. I walked the block briskly looking forward to seeing my wife and children again. When I rang the doorbell, no one was answering. No one was home. What a letdown? I sat down for a while and waited smoking a cigarette.

I sat on the steps for about an hour and a taxi pulled up, and out came my son Pel and my wife Doris. I hugged them all. It seemed like I had been gone for a lifetime. It was good to be home away from war, death, and typhoons.

[Chief Petty Officer (E7) Pelham (Ken) Kenneth Mead Jr. was officially discharged Nov. 3, 1945 from the U.S. Naval service. The nightmare on Okinawa was over, and WW II was over, and a new chapter at home was to begin.]

Prologue

It was 11 years later in December 1956 in Queens, New York. I was working as a linoleum mechanic putting down linoleum floors in Brooklyn, Queens, and Manhattan. I had just gotten home from work around 5:30 in the evening and my wife Doris was cooking dinner for the kids and I. As we sat down to dinner there was a knock at the door. I went down the stairs to answer the door. A tall Asian boy was standing in the doorway. I asked, "can I help you." The young man answered are you Ken san? All of a sudden a flash of memory came to mind and I recognized the expression but not the person. "Ken san, I am Asado, Sam boy from Okinawa," he said. I was shocked, Sam boy had grown up and here he was at my door step thousands of miles from Okinawa. I could not believe it. "Come in," I told him. Wow it is great to see you and how you have grown up? Come on upstairs and meet my family. We ate dinner and I told my family all the stories about Sam boy and his family in Okinawa and how we met and became friends. He reached into his jacket pocket and took out the Navy hat I had given him 11 years before. We talked all evening and I prepared the coach for him to sleep on that night. The next day we all had breakfast together and Sam boy felt he had found a family. He was going to New York University that day to enroll as a College student on a scholarship from the Asian Foundation of Okinawa. I wished him well as he left on the city bus for Manhattan. We hugged and he thanked me for saving his life in Okinawa and for the $20 American money I gave him. I told him he was family and to come and visit us on weekends when he had free time from his college studies. And so Sam boy came to visit on holidays. Our friendship grew and after four years he graduated from New York University. A new chapter in my life had begun and in Sam boy's life.

Appendix

Chronology of the Battle of Okinawa

April 1, 1945—Battle of Okinawa begins. Tenth Army lands on Higashi Beach. No Japs in sight—*Operation—Olympia.*

April 4, 1945—XXIV Corp of the Tenth Army makes first contact with Japanese defensive fortifications in Southern Okinawa.

April 6, 1945—the largest battleship ever built by the Japanese, the Yamato, was dispatched to Okinawa with no air cover. Carrying only enough fuel to reach Okinawa but not return. The American submarine Hackleback tracked her movements and alerted carrier-based bombers.

April 7, 1945—Vice Admiral Marc Mitscher launched air strikes at 10:00 a.m. The first hits were by the planes from the carrier Bennington and San Jacinto. Planes sunk the Japanese destroyer Hamakaze with a bomb and a torpedo hit. The light cruiser Yahagi was hit by bombs and went dead in the water. The Yahagi sank at 2:32 p.m. The Yamato took 12 bombs and 7 torpedo hits with two hours. Of the Yamato's crew of 2,747, only 23 officers and 246 enlisted men survived.

April 18, 1945—Pulitzer Prize winning newspaper columnist Ernie Pyle killed on Le Shima Island.

April 20, 1945—Kamikaze crashes into the aircraft carrier Bunker Hill.

May 13, 1945—Marines take Sugar Loaf Hill, which guards the entrance to Shuri Castle and the headquarters of the Japanese 32 Army.

May 24, 1945—Marines enter Nahu, capital of Okinawa, largest city taken by the Marines at that time on Okinawa.

June 10, 1945—Lt. General Simon B. Buckner, Jr., commanding the Tenth Army, offers surrender terms to Lt. Gen Ushijima Mitsuru, Commander of the 32 Imperial Japanese Army. No response is ever received.

June 15, 1945—Coordinated Japanese defense ends, and effectively the death of the 32nd Army.

June 18, 1945—Japanese artillery barrage kills Lt. General Buckner, Major General Roy Geiger USMC, assumes command of the Tenth Army; First Marine Officer to command a field army in combat.

June 21, 1945—Maj. General Geiger announces Okinawa Island secured

June 23, 1945—Gen. Ushijima and Lt. Gen Cho Isamu, Chief of staff of 32 Army, commit suicide at sunrise at the mouth of a cave in southern Okinawa. General Joseph W. Stilwell assumes command of the Tenth Army.

July 2, 1945—Mop up campaign finished. General Stilwell announces the Ryukus campaign terminated. End of 82-day campaign.

Antietam CVS-36 Aircraft Carrier Chronology

Aug.20, 1944—Antietam launched from Philadelphia shipyards.

Jan. 28, 1945—Antietam commissioned, Captain James R. Tague in Command.

May 19, 1945—Repairs completed and set course from Philadelphia to Norfolk. Stopped at Norfolk, Virginia three days.

May 20-23, 1945—Norfolk Naval Yards-stopover.

May 23, 1945—Set Course for Panama with Destroyer escorts Higbee (DD-806), George W. Ingram (Apd-43) and Ira Jeffery (APD-44).

May 31, 1945—Antietam arrived at Cristobal, Panama, Canal Zone.

June 1, 1945—Transited Panama Canal.

June 10-13, 1945—Antietam stopped at San Diego en route to Hawaii.

June 19—Antietam arrives in Pearl Harbor and commences training missions until

June 20—Antietam war exercises in Pear Harbor.

Aug. 4—Antietam steaming toward Guam to join the Pacific fleet.

Aug. 6—First Atomic Bomb dropped on Hiroshima at 8:15 a.m.

Aug. 9—Second Atomic Bomb dropped on Nagasaki.

Aug. 9—Soviet Union invades Manchuria.

Aug.11—False announcement that War said to be over at 6:45.

Aug. 12—Antietam left Pearl Harbor—Set course for western Pacific area.

Aug. 13—Crossed the International dateline at 1900.

Aug. 14—War said to be over at 12:15 officially.

Aug. 15—Three days out of Oahu, received word of Japanese capitulation, and the consequent cessation of hostilities.

Aug. 19th—Arrive Eniwetok Atoll, Marshall Islands-mission changed from combat to Occupation support duty. Anchored alongside the aircraft carrier, Interpid. Aug. 21st-Antietam set course at 0628 with a Task Force consisting of U.S.S. Intrepid (CV-11) U.S.S. Cabot (CVL-28), U.S.S. Kimberly ((DD-521), U.S.S. Halsey Powell (DD-686), U.S.S. Allen M. Sumner (DD-692, U.S.S. Obrien (DD-725), U.S.S. Robert t. Hunington (DD-781) and U.S.S. Myles C. Fox (DD-692) a screen of destroyers bound for Japan. AA gunnery exercises were conducted from 0852 to 1255 at the conclusion of exercises the task force came to course at 20 knots. Plans were for this task unit to rendezvous with Task Force 38 about 225 miles Southeast of Tokyo. Anchors aweigh at 0630. Set course for Tokyo Bay via the Marcus and Moke islands to join Task Force 38.

Aug. 23. 1945—at 23:25 in accordance with orders from Com. Third Fleet, U.S.S. Antietam, U.S.S. Ringold, and U.S.S. Harrison, left formation with orders to proceed to GUAM. The Antietam CVS-36 suffered some internal damage, which forced her to sail to the port at Apra Harbor, GUAM for inspections.

Aug. 26—pulled into Guam for inspection

*The inspection party deemed the damage minimal and the carrier remained operational and can return to her course on Aug. 27th.

Aug. 25 at 0500 impending typhoon in the Tokyo Bay area.

Aug. 27th—Antietam CVS-36 Left Guan for Okinawa, and in route receives orders to change course to coast of Asian mainland rather than proceed to Tokyo Harbor.

Aug. 30th—Anchors at Okinawa Aug. 29—Antietam arrives at 14:30 at Okinawa, secured General Quarters at 1822 to dusk. Ship darkened with numerous small boat patrols stationed off the beach. U.S.S. Ringgold, and U.S.S. Harrison accompanied Antietam into the harbor berthing.

Aug. 30, 1945—Chief Petty Office Ken Mead and four other sailors get off at Okinawa.

Sept.1, 1945—Antietam sets course for waters near Shanghai, China at 06:30.

Sept. 2· 1945—Peace treaty signed by Japanese on the U.S.S. Missouri in Tokyo Bay, Japan.

Sept. 2, 1945 U.S.S. Antietam Arrives in Chinese waters near Shanghai.

Sept. 7, 1945—censorship of the mail lifted.

Sept 11, 1945—U.S.S. Antietam sets course for Shanghai, China.

Sept. 13, 1945—U.S.S. Antietam arrives back at Okinawa again.

Sept. 15, 1945—*Typhoon coming* and hangar deck of U.S.S. Antietam shipping water.

Sept 17, 1945—Typhoon still rough.

Sept. 22, 1945 Beer party on Okinawa crew of the U.S.S. Antietam

Sept. 27, 1945 U.S.S. Antietam left Okinawa.

Oct. 2, 1945—U.S.S. Antietam refuels tanker at sea.

Oct. 5, 1945—U.S.S. Antietam at Anchor in Yellow Sea.

CPSIA information can be obtained at www.ICGtesting.com
Printed in the USA
LVOW131253160413

329270LV00003B/343/P